A Force Stronger than Anything She'd Known

made her turn her head to where Vince was gazing at her. It was a moment out of time, when no one else existed for either of them. It was a look that told her there was nothing on earth that could keep them apart if he wanted her . . . and he *wanted* her.

Julia gave a sudden shiver as the music ended. But it wasn't the cold that made her shiver. It was a fever that gripped her, a fever that would consume her if she didn't get away from it soon. . . .

JEAN SAUNDERS
describes herself as a compulsive writer and has written 23 novels and over 600 short stories. A participating member of several British writers' organizations, including the Romantic Novelists Association, Jean enjoys anything to do with writing and writers.

Dear Reader:

During the last year, many of you have written to Silhouette telling us what you like best about Silhouette Romances and, more recently, about Silhouette Special Editions. You've also told us what else you'd like to read from Silhouette. With your comments and suggestions in mind, we've developed SILHOUETTE DESIRE.

SILHOUETTE DESIREs will be on sale this June, and each month we'll bring you four new DESIREs written by some of your favorite authors—Stephanie James, Diana Palmer, Rita Clay, Suzanne Simms and many more.

SILHOUETTE DESIREs may not be for everyone, but they are for those readers who want a more sensual, provocative romance. The heroines are slightly older—women who are actively involved in their careers and the world around them. If you want to experience all the excitement, passion and joy of falling in love, then SILHOUETTE DESIRE is for you.

I'd appreciate any thoughts you'd like to share with us on new SILHOUETTE DESIRE, and I invite you to write to us at the address below:

Editor-in-Chief,
Silhouette Books,
330 Steelcase Road East,
Markham, Ontario L3R 2M1

JEAN SAUNDERS
The Kissing Time

Silhouette *Romance*

Published by Silhouette Books New York

Distributed in Canada by PaperJacks Ltd., a Licensee
of the trademarks of Simon & Schuster, a division of
Gulf+Western Corporation.

SILHOUETTE BOOKS, a Simon & Schuster Division of
GULF & WESTERN CORPORATION
1230 Avenue of the Americas, New York, N.Y. 10020
In Canada distributed by PaperJacks Ltd.,
330 Steelcase Road, Markham, Ontario.

Distributed by Pocket Books

ISBN: 0-671-57149-4

First Silhouette Books printing May, 1982

10 9 8 7 6 5 4 3 2 1

America's Publisher of Contemporary Romance

Printed in Canada

Chapter One

There was definitely something to be said for being alone with the elements, Julia decided. The mellow autumn breeze lifted the weight of her long glossy dark hair from her slim shoulders, and sent the fragrance of gorse and bracken to her nostrils, along with the pure clean scent of Scottish air.

Julia had always felt a great affinity with Scotland, and the romantic highlands in particular. It took only a slight stretching of the imagination to visualise the men who had been her ancestors striding through the heather in kilt and tam-o'-shanter, with the plaintive skirl of the bagpipes lingering on the balmy air, echoing and re-echoing as the sounds merged into the circle of blue-hazed mountains, and complemented by the gurgle of rushing waterfalls.

She paused in her climb to the top of the ridge of hills overlooking her aunt's cottage and gazed all around her slowly. It was like something out of a film set, she thought with a catch in her breath; colourful, motionless, perfect. Away to the foothills of the mountains stretched vast tracts of heather-carpeted slopes. The only sounds were the rustling of leaves and the call of a bird to its mate high among fluffy white puffball clouds in a pale blue sky. The vastness of space had an oddly beneficial effect on her, the way it always had. . . .

For a few seconds Julia closed her expressive eyes against the dazzle of yellow gorse and gave an unconscious small shiver. Despite her resolution to put the past behind her, where it belonged, there were still moments when Martin's voice would be unbearably, heartbreakingly near, as if he stood just behind her shoulder, ready to take her in his arms the minute she turned round.

"You know what they say about gorse, don't you, darling?" he'd tease her. "When the gorse is in bloom, it's kissing time. And since it's always in bloom somewhere or other . . ."

Julia turned quickly, but the voice was only in her head, the sighing of the breeze. She watched the birds as they soared high into the sky for a moment longer, and then began to pick her way carefully back to Aunt Meg's cottage, her control firmly secure again.

For such a petite young woman, Julia Chase was extraordinarily strong-willed and resilient. Blessedly so, since she'd had more than enough upheaval to cope with for a girl of twenty years old on the brink of marriage. Six months ago, she'd considered herself a girl who had everything: a fascinating job that she loved, and a fiancé who adored her. Added to that she was a strikingly lovely girl, with pale, delicate skin in direct contrast to the glossy chestnut hair and the unexpectedness of eyes the colour of wood violets. Her face was a perfect heart-shape, and the full mobile mouth made her beautiful when she smiled and gave added animation to an already appealing personality. Her nose was neat, as was the rest of her, her overall shape soft and rounded. And not the least part of Julia's attractiveness was the soft Cornish voice, as rich as Cornish cream.

Six months ago, she'd expected to be Mrs. Martin Tregorran within a few weeks of Easter, and to have spent the summer as a bride. Everything had been arranged, and it was all going to be so perfect . . . almost too perfect, she had sometimes thought a little tremulously, as if no two people had any right to such happiness . . . and she had been right to feel that way, because with only three weeks to go until the wedding, Martin's car had been involved in a horrific pileup on the M4 motorway. And somewhere in the tangled wreckage of the lorry and the family cars had been Martin's two-seater, soft-topped and vulnerable. He hadn't stood a chance.

Julia stumbled a little in the long, knee-length boots into which she'd tucked her jeans to go climbing the hillside. Even in the warm yellow sweater she shivered a little with the pain of remembering, and she pushed the memories deliberately away from her as she neared her aunt's cottage. Sometimes she wanted to hold them close to her for precious moments, but the sensible part of her told her it was pointless and painful, because they only brought the ache of losing Martin searingly close again, like the shock of iced water thrown in her face.

She usually managed to control the rush of emotions that still hit her head-on when she least expected them, and she had managed to construct a glass wall between herself and anyone who tried to get too close to her, unable yet to think of another man touching her the way Martin had, or loving her with the promise of the sweet wild abandon that had been so cruelly snatched away from her. Never again, she had vowed. Martin was still too real to her for her to want to expose her emotions so freely again. She was still too emotionally involved with him, even if she could no longer see him, and she wasn't the sort who could love lightly. He'd told her that when the gorse was in bloom it was kissing time . . . in the language of flowers gorse stood for constancy, too. . . .

In the end, Julia knew she had to get away from

Cornwall and all the familiar places that still held Martin's image too vividly, even if it meant giving up the absorbing job with Mr. Pollard, who was beginning to resemble the antiques in which he dealt. She knew she'd miss the excitement of the big auctions in the old English country houses, of touring junkyards, of having some dear old soul step diffidently into the antique shop with some small piece she'd been hoarding as a keepsake, and sometimes discovering it was excitingly valuable. A "find," in Mr. Pollard's words. She'd miss it all . . . but the move had to be made, and she knew it.

And in Aunt Meg's cottage at Strathrowan, among the Scottish hills, there was always a ready welcome. Even though she hadn't been here since she was a child, the interior of the cottage had been surprisingly vivid to Julia. It had been a little like stepping back into childhood to be back in the tiny, oil-lit rooms with their quaintly pungent smell of paraffin and well-waxed furniture; the solid oak pieces and chintz-covered chairs, and even the old rag-type rugs on the floor she remembered Aunt Meg working on years ago, were still bright and serviceable.

And Aunt Meg herself—greyer and a wee bit smaller than Julia remembered—with her quick bird-like movements and bustling ways. The kind of woman who was the salt of the earth. She was of tough Murdy stock, she never tired of saying proudly, and added that the Murdy blood ran in Julia's veins, too, which was how she'd known she'd be a survivor, despite everything.

Julia was beginning to believe it was true. She'd been here a week now, and already she could look back at the hillside, ablaze with purple and blue, and the patches of yellow gorse so reminiscent of Cornwall and the moors she had loved, without quite such an agonising tug at her emotions. It was the same and yet different. It wasn't the kissing time anymore.

She was beginning to accept it, and imperceptibly her heart was beginning to heal. . . .

Her footsteps brought her to the stony lane alongside the cottage. It sat, squat and businesslike, in the hamlet of Strathrowan, its old stonework glinting in the afternoon sunlight. She pushed open the white-painted door and mouthed hello as she saw Aunt Meg talking animatedly on the telephone. The cottage might be remote, but Aunt Meg had a constant flow of phone calls, Julia thought with amusement. She went into the tiny kitchen to make some tea, and a few minutes later her aunt joined her, the perfect country woman in thick Arran-knit jumper and tweed skirt, in complete contrast to Julia's bright yellow sweater and tight-fitting denims.

"That was Rose Galbraith," Aunt Meg announced. "She's an old friend—an Englishwoman who married into the Galbraith family."

Julia hid a smile. However fond her aunt might be of Rose Galbraith, the other lady would always be "an Englishwoman who married into . . ." Aunt Meg was passionately Scottish.

"I told Rose you were here on a visit, Julia. She rang to invite me to a little dinner party, and she included you in the invitation at once, of course. I haven't seen her for nearly a year because she's been abroad on one of her frequent trips. I don't know why she doesn't admit to being a world traveller and leave Galbraith Hall in the capable hands of her son. You'll love the Hall, Julia. I think there's a newspaper cutting somewhere . . ."

She disappeared into the parlour and Julia heard her rummaging in a drawer while she finished making the tea and carried it through on a tray. She poured them each a cup and took the newspaper cutting from her aunt's hand with a smile.

It showed a fine old country house set in spacious grounds. The house itself was large, and obviously belonged to a wealthy family. The setting was even more impressive than the house itself though. Set on the slope of a hillside, the mountains towered gloriously behind it like protective guardians, and the whole estate was fringed by tall, dark pine trees. Julia had a swift image of how it would look in winter, the mountains snow-capped as they soared into the mists, the trees spangled in the morning sunlight like a thousand garlanded Christmas trees. Having been in plenty of similar estates on her job, Julia was impressed but not overawed. In the foreground of the photo a handsome, dark-haired man with a strong face knelt beside a shaggy dog. Even in the newsprint photo Julia could see the arrogant tilt to the man's head and the look of seeming to own the world coming from confident, piercing dark eyes. . . .

"That's Vince, Rose's son," Aunt Meg was saying now. "It's not often he'll let Galbraith Hall be photographed, but there was some charity affair that day, so he was probably on his best behaviour. He's more likely to tell the reporters to get lost than let them in when they turn up casually looking for a story to print." She chuckled. "Vince is never short of words when he needs them."

Julia was hardly listening. Her heart thudded painfully. Vincent Galbraith looked thirtyish in the photo, and probably what in England would be called "County"—in other words, an unbearable snob. Not her type at all . . . and yet there was a certain something about him in the newsprint photo . . . maybe it was the way the wind was ruffling his dark hair, making him look more boyish than he really was. Or the twinkle in those dark eyes as he fondled the head of the shaggy dog . . . despite the twinkle, Julia could imagine the same eyes becoming hard and ruthless if he didn't get his own way, and the undeniably sensual mouth tightening with anger if his privacy was invaded. . . .

And yet, despite all of that, the boyish look superseded all those things, and as she looked at the photo she felt an explosion of emotions inside her. It was almost as if she knew the man already . . . yet even stronger than that was the fact that she didn't *want* to know him, or see him, because he had such a look of Martin about him that it churned up everything she'd been trying so hard to control.

Julia told herself she was being ridiculous, and studied the house instead of the man. Vince Galbraith was probably nothing at all like Martin. What added to the illusion was the fact that Martin had had a high roll-neck sweater just like the one Vince Galbraith wore so elegantly over his broad shoulders.

Next day she told Aunt Meg she was going for her usual walk in the hills. The cottage was so tiny it was good to get away from each other now and then. It had been a crofter's cottage a century ago, belonging to a hardy hillman who'd tended his sheep on the steep slopes and coaxed his solitary crops from the garden in which Aunt Meg now grew herbs and shrubs. The whole area gave Julia a sense of continuity that could always soothe her ragged nerves.

She struck out across the narrow track leading to her favourite ridge. The wind sighed softly through the bracken, and clouds floated silently over the distant peaks, swallowing them up in a cotton-wool drift. She walked for an hour, past small wooden huts and storm fences that told their own story of harsher seasons, when the local farmers guarded their livestock as best they could, and by the time she returned to the cottage the fresh air had whipped up a fine glow in her pale cheeks, and a sparkle in her violet eyes, and Julia knew the hills had somehow worked their special magic again.

As she reached the cottage, she saw the familiar uniformed postman getting back in his van and driving off. Aunt Meg had just opened a square white envelope and was waving an invitation card under Julia's nose.

"I told you about the Galbraiths' dinner party! Rose never could do anything simply. A phone call would have been enough, but no, it had to be done elaborately, as usual." There was laughter and affection in her voice as she handed the card over to Julia to read.

It was very ornate. It had the Galbraith coat of arms impressed in gilt at the top, and the lettering was so flowery that it wasn't readily legible unless read slowly. All intended to create an illusion of grandeur, Julia thought cynically.

"Tomorrow night!" she exclaimed when she saw the date on the card. "They don't give us much notice, do they?"

Aunt Meg laughed. "That's Rose! She just assumes everyone will drop any previous plans when she gives the command. And people usually do. The whole family has a charisma about them, and their dinner parties are legendary. They always invite an interesting group of people who'll mix well together."

It sounded too clinical. Julia was almost beginning to dislike them before she'd met them, despite Aunt Meg's obvious affection for her old friend. And "the whole family"? She'd only heard mention of one son, Vince, and the sudden image of the arrogant, worldly look in those dark eyes, and the wide, sensual mouth, swept forcibly into her mind.

"How many of them are there, then?" she asked quickly, aware that her heart was doing its strange jungle dance again.

"Rose is a widow now, and an extremely intelligent woman. She rules the roost at the Hall. Then there's Vince, who's just about the most eligible bachelor for miles. The two younger children Rose always calls her afterthoughts because they were born in quick succession when Vince was already a young teen-ager. James must be fifteen now, and Fern a year younger. Rose used to travel a lot in the old days with her husband, so the young ones have very mature heads on their shoulders from relying on a rather stern Nanny, the housekeeper, and an older brother to keep them in check."

Julia thought they sounded a pretty formidable lot, and was vaguely sorry for the "afterthoughts." Despite her earlier reluctance to meet the arrogant Vincent, she was growing more and more intrigued by the sound of the Galbraiths. And maybe he wasn't as arrogant as he looked. . . .

Her mind sidetracked to what to wear for the occasion. Should one sport a Scottish tartan and claim kinship to one of the clans for entry to the house? Did the Murdys even *have* a tartan? There was an Innes connection way back in her ancestry, and they certainly did . . . the Innes clan went back as far as the twelfth century. She'd looked up the clan motto once—Be Traist was the Gaelic phrase, which in English meant be trusting. . . .

"What are you smiling so wickedly about?" Aunt Meg's voice broke into her thoughts just as she was thinking she'd never particularly trusted a man who had looks and wealth and charisma besides, so Vince Galbraith was due for the thumbs down from the start, wondering, too, if she should rush down to Glasgow to find a shop selling some authentic Highland rig to impress the imperious Galbraiths. *No way,* she told herself determinedly.

"Nothing at all," she said airily. "But I suppose there's no need to dig out the family tiaras for the occasion, is there?"

Aunt Meg gave a sudden little laugh. "My dear girl, I hope I haven't made them sound like royalty! Any little dress will do, and nothing *too* formal.

13

Anyway, whatever you wear, you'll be the belle of the ball, while I shall look my usual homely self even if I'm dripping in diamonds!"

Julia grinned. She'd already decided what to wear. She travelled prepared for anything, and she was glad she wouldn't be disgracing Aunt Meg by letting these Galbraiths think she was just a little country girl who wouldn't know a cocktail dress from a sheepskin jacket.

She'd wear a silky little black dress with a low-gathered neckline and shoe-string straps, its starkness relieved by the shimmer of silver trimming along the fluted hemline. To go with it, there was a gossamer silvery stole and silver sandals with elegant high heels to give added height to her five feet two inches. She would pile her dark hair on top of her head in big loose curls with long tendrils at the sides to add to the illusion. The effect, Martin had told her when he'd seen her with her hair up for the first time, had been positively stunning. Julia caught her breath at the sudden sweet memory. . . .

"Don't worry, I won't let you down," she told Aunt Meg quickly.

"I never thought for a moment that you would. Now, how do you fancy starting our meal while I put my feet up for five minutes? You're always telling me what a good cook you were in that bed-sitter of yours—and you don't think I invited you up here merely to be decorative, do you? There's lamb cutlets and roasties for tonight."

Her voice was brisk in its no-nonsense Scottish accent as she noted the sudden shine in Julia's lovely eyes and guessed the reason. But Julia did as she was asked, knowing she'd been sent to the kitchen to keep her hands and her thoughts busy. A few seconds later the phone rang again, and she grinned as she heard her aunt's animated tones. So much for taking a wee rest!

"That was Rose again," Aunt Meg announced

behind her in a little while. "She's suggested that we go to Galbraith Hall early in the day tomorrow for you to take a good look round, and then stay on for a couple of days. It's been so long since I've seen her, I'm afraid I just agreed without thinking whether you'd prefer to stay here, love. If you'd rather I rang back and changed the arrangements . . ."

"No, of course you mustn't do that! It'll be very nice to see how the other half lives." Julia hoped she didn't sound as tongue-in-cheek as she felt. One dinner party would have been enough . . . but Aunt Meg looked relieved at her reply.

"You'll love the place, I know. It's a very old house, full of such lovely things, and just up your street, I should think, Julia. And you must get Vince to tell you about the Galbraith ghost, too."

She looked at her Aunt sharply. "You haven't said anything about—"

"Martin? No, dear. I've merely said my niece had come to stay for a few weeks while she's between jobs. That's all they know about you except that you've come from Cornwall. I know that's the way you wanted it."

"That's right," Julia said firmly.

She guessed Aunt Meg would have liked to confide everything in her old friend, Rose Galbraith, and it was pure luck that she'd been out of the country while the worst few months of Julia's life were happening. The last thing she wanted now was for the usual look of sympathy and embarrassment to appear whenever anyone discovered the truth about her tragedy. . . .

Now, of course, she thought ruefully, the Galbraiths would probably think she was the frivolous sort, if Aunt Meg's "between jobs" remark had been taken seriously! Maybe even a fortune hunter, and eager to set eyes on such an eligible bachelor as Vince Galbraith was reputed to be!

It seemed impossible that she'd never even heard

of this man until last night, Julia thought irritably, when he seemed to be taking up so much of her thinking time. And now she had no option but to spend a few days in his house.

After their meal of succulent Scottish lamb cutlets and golden brown roasties with plenty of mint sauce to pep them up, they sorted out the clothes to take to Galbraith Hall. Take plenty, was Aunt Meg's advice. The weather was changeable at present, and Galbraith Hall was high beyond the Kilpatrick Hills, where the nights could cool rapidly.

"It's a very beautiful part of the country," she told her niece. "Right in the old Galbraith clan stronghold, and with a fabulous view of Loch Lomond. All very romantic, and no matter what time of year, the loch is beautiful. I don't think you've ever seen it, have you, Julia?"

"No, I haven't." Romantic settings weren't high on her list of priorities at the moment. But then, she didn't have to look at it. . . . There was a stirring of interest for the "lovely things" in Galbraith Hall. Her training in the antique business gave her endless pleasure when left to her own devices in a country house.

"How old is Galbraith Hall?" she asked now.

"Oh, I'm not sure. There's a tale that Bonnie Prince Charlie took refuge there at one time, so if that's true then the house must have been standing before 1745. No one really knows the truth of it, and many old Scottish houses like to boast that the prince slept there. Certainly, he had a victory during a battle at Falkirk in 1746, which isn't so far away, so it's possible that Galbraith Hall was a refuge. It's a pretty story to imagine that the Lad Born to be King once occupied a corner of your house, but it would be hard to find the truth of it now."

Such tales had always intrigued Julia, and by the time they set out the following morning in her aunt's old Ford, she was actually looking forward to seeing Galbraith Hall.

It was a long winding route, through narrow roads with passing places for traffic, and they often had to stop for stocky Highland cattle or slow-stepping long-haired sheep, who looked at them blankly. Occasionally a shepherd would raise his crook in greeting, or touch his tam-o'-shanter. It was pure Hollywood, Julia thought dreamily, and she loved it, from the clear tumbling burns to the splendours of grey-sheened turreted castles and the lowliest thatched cottages.

When they finally turned on to a narrow road leading up to a large, imposing building of granite stone and ivy-coloured walls, Julia felt a surge of anticipation inside.

"Some place, eh?" Aunt Meg said prosaically as they entered the tall iron gates and drove through a shrub-lined driveway to the heavy front door.

"You can say that again," Julia said drily. Not that such places were foreign to her. She'd been in too many of them, but never as a house guest. To enjoy its atmosphere as those old ghosts must have done. Ghosts to her weren't the creepy, chain-dragging variety, or the hazy visions floating through walls so beloved of TV plays. They were the essence of old places, the distant echoes of the past that had shaped the future of a building such as this one.

They were shown to the drawing room, where Mrs. Galbraith and morning coffee awaited them. Julia's eyes widened with delight as she saw the elegant furnishings of silk and brocade, the beautiful porcelain on little tables and in japanned cabinets, the richly patterned carpets and paintings discreetly lit to show the colours off to best advantage. Clearly Mrs. Galbraith was a collector of taste, and not quite as formidable as Julia might have expected.

She accepted the china coffee cup from the

straight-backed Rose Galbraith with a smile. Mrs. Galbraith wore an impeccably tailored tweed suit and pearls round her neck. Her smile was fixed politely on her carefully made-up face. Her eyes were exactly like the eyes of her son in the newspaper cutting, Julia thought instantly. Dark and somewhat remote until she smiled, and capable of cutting you into little pieces with one freezing glance if she chose to do so.

For a moment, Julia felt as if she were under a microscope as Rose gave her a sweeping assessment with those piercing eyes. Maybe Rose was used to young ladies eyeing the place—and her eligible son—with a view to moving in, and wondered if her friend's niece was of similar inclination. She needn't worry on that score, but it was hardly something Julia could convey in the first five minutes of arriving here!

She was imagining old Mr. Pollard's delight at seeing such treasures obviously cared for and used lovingly. Mrs. Galbraith followed her appreciative eyes to a large blue vase on a side table, set with panels of exotic birds and flowers.

"I see you admire beautiful things, Julia," she commented. "It's English Worcester, you know."

"Yes, I do know. Dr. Wall Worcester, isn't it?"

The words tripped out easily, and Rose suddenly stared, as if realising that this lovely young niece of her old friend had a clever head on her shoulders. Beauty as well as brains. . . .

"Now tell me how you knew that?" Rose commanded.

Julia laughed a little self-consciously. She hadn't intended to start airing her knowledge, and the remark had been made involuntarily.

"By the faint greenish look of the porcelain, and the way the glaze has shrunk just a little at the edges here." She indicated what she meant. "That's no detriment to its value, but it's a dead giveaway to the expert."

"Oh, dear, Rose, I should have warned you that Julia *is* quite an expert." Aunt Meg laughed at the astonishment on her friend's face. "She'll be itching to have a look round if I know her!"

Rose's smile held more warmth in it this time. "Then so she must. If you've finished your coffee, my dear, feel free to explore wherever you wish. I'm sure you'll find a good deal to interest you. The library is at the end of this hall, and as well as many rare books, there are some fine paintings on the walls. The desk in the study next door is Chippendale. Remind me to ask Vincent to show you the original bill for its purchase, which, I'm sure, will be of interest. But no doubt you'll be able to tell us more than we know ourselves when you've had a browse around."

Julia replaced her coffee cup with a feeling of relief as she left the two friends together to chat. As she closed the door she heard Mrs. Galbraith tell her aunt that Julia was going to be a great surprise to Vince. Why that should be, she couldn't imagine, and cared even less.

The next hour was one of sheer delight for her. She made her way through all the ground floor rooms, almost dazzled by the wealth of elegant pieces of furniture and costly porcelain, the bric-a-brac which in itself might be worth very little, but when massed together in a collection were very valuable indeed. The Galbraiths were canny Scots, if such pieces had been chosen for their intrinsic personal appeal only, and without knowledge of their collective value.

There was a smaller version of the drawing room, carpeted in pale gold with complementary wallpaper. It had little feminine touches: a firescreen near the old stone fireplace, and a small collection of lace and ebony fans inside a little glass case. She guessed this would once have been a ladies' sewing room, with the morning sunlight striking directly on a small table at the window. On the table now though, instead of the Victorian ladies' embroidery equipment, was a delicate fine glass bowl, embellished with a tracery of trellliswork like the icing on a cake.

Her fingers sought for the telltale Ravenscroft seal—the small dab of glass bearing the raven's head in relief—and she smiled ruefully when she failed to find it. It was unlikely. Such truly authentic pieces were rare, indeed, but she'd still guess that this was genuine Ravenscroft, or else a brilliant fake. . . .

"I hope you realise that the object you're holding is very valuable," a strong male voice with a pronounced Scottish accent spoke right behind her. If Julia hadn't been so used to handling items of such value, the shock of hearing someone else in the room when she'd thought she was alone might have made her drop the dish. As it was, she replaced it carefully on its plinth before she whirled quickly, expecting to see the man who'd shown them into the house, and reacting before she had time to think.

"And if I hadn't known that very well, it might easily have been in a thousand pieces by now, with you surprising me like that!" she snapped, and then her face flooded with colour as she recognised instantly the tall figure of Vincent Galbraith lounging against the door which he'd closed silently behind him. She knew him at once from his photo in the newspaper cutting, but in the flesh he was even more of a man than she had expected.

The Laird of Galbraith, the thought flashed through her mind. And looking every inch of it, from the top of his unruly dark hair and those insolent eyes, to the unsmiling, sensual mouth that was pursed together now at her reply, as if hardly able to believe that anyone had turned on him with such a retort in this house where he was king. Julia found herself forming an instant image of the man, as if her mind felt obliged to register a photographic impression that would linger long after they parted.

He wore a black shirt that was open halfway to his waist, so that she could see the dark hair on his broad chest. Light-coloured slacks tapered over his slim hips. He was a man who oozed sensuality, and knew how to use it to the best effect. His unexpected appearance had set her nerve-ends tingling and her heart thumping, and she was angry with him for making her feel like an intruder eyeing the family treasures. She wondered just how long he had stood there watching her, for she had been so engrossed in the Ravenscroft piece she had heard nothing of his arrival, especially since he wore soft sneakers on his feet. No doubt to add to the sporty, virile effect, she thought scornfully.

She was suddenly aware that he had stopped looking at her as if she had no right to be here. Instead, the dark eyes, that she realised now had little golden flecks in them when they were caught by the reflected sunlight, flickered with a new interest as they took in the taut lines of her body as she stood there defensively. She had worn a lime green blouse and denim skirt for travelling, and it was a blouse that clung tightly to her figure, moulding her soft curves.

She saw Vince's glance rest on them for a moment that seemed like a year. It was a look that seemed to strip her naked, and made her feel like putting her hands across herself. He had no right to make her feel that way, Julia thought angrily. His gaze moved slowly downward, past the neat little waist and the feminine flare of her hips to the slim legs that ended in strappy green sandals. He leaned back against the door, his eyes returning to her face after what seemed like an eternity.

"And why shouldn't I appear in my own home to

query a stranger?" he challenged. "Or is it the done thing in England to wander about where you will in someone else's house, examining the expensive pieces of glassware?"

"Of course not!" Julia felt her face redden even more as the cool gaze continued to assess her. "I was merely admiring the beautiful things you have in Galbraith Hall as I was invited to, Mr. Galbraith—"

"Ah, so you know who I am. And from your delightful accent, I take it you're the little Cornish niece Meggie's been keeping up her sleeve all this time." His voice was condescending, whether he meant it to be or not.

"I assure you that whatever you may have expected, we are not all besotted with folklore in Cornwall, nor do we walk about with hayseeds at the corners of our mouths," she was nettled enough to reply. She forced herself to remember that she was a guest in his house, and put a tight little smile on her lips as she finished speaking, but inwardly she was seething.

Aunt Meg had said the whole family had a charisma about them, but this particular Galbraith had more arrogance than she'd ever met in a man before. It oozed out of him as he lounged against the door. She'd met his type before, of course. They thought they owned the world and everything in it . . . and Vince had a sardonic gleam in his eyes now. He hadn't missed the sarcasm in her voice.

"What a shame. It would have been interesting to uncover some secrets of the Cornish piskies from one of the natives. Shall we begin again and introduce ourselves properly? You're Julia, of course."

It was obvious that he was going to be ultrapolite to his guest now, though to Julia it just seemed patronising. She had turned away from him and when she turned to face Vince Galbraith again her heart gave an unexpected little jolt.

The sardonic expression had lessened, and the smile was more natural, if still as forced as her own.

But he no longer looked broodingly angry, and now she felt the full force of the Galbraith charm. Intentional or not, it seemed to reach out and engulf her. Vince's eyes were dark and warm when they weren't flashing with anger, the wide mouth parted to show strong white teeth in his ruggedly tanned face. Julia had a job not to catch her breath as his hand reached out for hers in a formal handshake.

He was very tall, and she felt dwarfed by his presence, but it was more than that. Perhaps it was her Cornish feyness that told her this was a momentous meeting, whether she wanted it that way or not. There was no other logical explanation for the tingles running through her at his touch, and she almost snatched her hand away from him. . . .

Chapter Two

The small hint of condescension and the knowledge that her accent had given her away so convincingly made Julia snap out of her trancelike moment. He had a nerve, she thought, her violet eyes sparkling with annoyance. He'd managed to embarrass her right off, and it was a good thing she was completely unsusceptible to Vince Galbraith's brand of animal magnetism, or she'd have been a shivering jelly by now. It was probably the way most other girls reacted, she thought witheringly, but not this one! She lifted her chin.

"And you're the son who 'manages the estate,' are you?" She managed to make it sound like a part-time occupation to convey the opinion that pampered sons of rich, doting mothers would be better off put down at birth like unwanted kittens.

"That would seem to bother you," he said curtly. "I'd almost forgotten that people such as yourself, buried in a quaint rustic backwater, wouldn't agree with the idea of a more feudal ancestry. Would you rather the whole of the British Isles was peopled with fisher-folk?"

He was too much, she raged! "Are you always this offensive to guests in your house?" she snapped.

"Or is it an honour specially reserved for me? Aunt Meg should have warned me I was entering the home of Scottish nobility. I'd have remembered to pack my tiara!"

To her complete surprise, Vince started to laugh. He was the most unpredictable man. He left her weak with his quicksilver changes of mood.

"I think you and I are going to get along very well, Julia. I like a girl who's not afraid to stand up to me when I get on my soapbox—providing she comes round to my way of thinking in the end, of course."

"Really?" she said crossly. "I doubt if I'll be around long enough to get on well with you or anyone. My stay with Aunt Meg is only intended to be temporary."

She felt bleak for a moment. She spoke the truth, but where she would go from here she had no idea. In a bizarre way, clashing with Vince Galbraith had at least taken her mind off her own unhappiness for a few moments, but this pompous young man was clearly obsessed with his own importance, and the less she saw of him the better.

How she could ever have imagined he bore the slightest resemblance to Martin she couldn't think. They weren't in the least alike. Martin had been a very gentle person, while this man was aggressively masculine, and those mercurial changes of mood were unnerving to say the least.

He was shrugging now, as if he couldn't care less whether she stayed in Scotland or not.

"Would you excuse me, please?" Julia said stiffly. "I'd like to take a look round the grounds, and I find it rather stifling in here."

It was a corny line, but she hoped he took her meaning. He needled her quicker than anyone she'd ever met, and she flicked her long hair away from her shoulders with an oddly defensive gesture as she passed him. He held the door open in an exaggerated gesture, and his arm brushed hers. It was the lightest of touches, yet the small contact seemed to burn like fire through the thin material of her blouse, sending little shock waves of awareness through her that took her completely by surprise. She almost fled out the door, and then stood helplessly, not sure which way to take through the many twisting corridors of the ground floor.

Vince was right behind her. His voice was mocking now. "Rose said you'd probably be lost by now. I'd originally come looking for you. I was curious to see this paragon that Meggie's been talking about so enthusiastically, and I'd already volunteered to show you the grounds. This way!"

He strode off before she could think of a suitable retort. He was clearly used to having people obey him when he spoke. She watched the smooth undulating movements of his hips as he moved away from her, a real anger inside her. And something else, too. There was a grudging admiration for his style . . . he was arrogant, too self-assured . . . all the things she despised in a son of the landed gentry . . . but he certainly had style.

And she *did* want to see the grounds. Julia swallowed her pride and hurried after him. Once outside the house, Vince still walked ahead with his long stride until she slowed down perversely. She could never keep up with him unless he waited for her. When he reached a small rhododendron thicket beyond the formal gardens, he turned and watched her approach. She stumbled a little as her heels sank into the spongy earth.

"You could have chosen better footwear." His voice was cool as he looked down at the lime-green sandals through which her pink-tipped toes peeped, already touched with damp earth and leaves. It was obvious to her at this moment that he considered her and this whole visit a complete nuisance.

"I didn't expect to be tramping through a mini-jungle," she retorted. And suddenly she remembered the way Martin used to tease her about her weakness for pretty, ridiculous shoes, no matter what the weather. Her soft red lips trembled, and she found herself biting them quickly. Such sweet memories had a habit of catching her unawares. . . .

Vince misconstrued her reaction to his curt comment, unaware of the true reason for it, and looked momentarily embarrassed. His voice was rough as he spoke. "My dear girl, I was only teasing you! It makes no difference to me if you want to tramp about in underwater flippers!"

For a second he put his hand on her shoulder and gave it a squeeze, and his words died away as he felt her stiffen at his touch. Julia saw his surprise, and guessed that he wasn't used to this reaction. Nor to the fact that there was a sudden look of withdrawal in her lovely violet eyes at his touch. Since Martin had died, she had felt this repugnance when any man touched her, but she was willing to bet that not many girls reacted that way in Vince Galbraith's company! His hand dropped from her shoulder at once.

"I apologise, Miss Chase—or should it be 'chaste?' " he said freezingly. "Someone should have warned me that Cornish girls don't like to be touched. It makes them unique in my experience! How the dickens did Meggie ever come to have such a prickly niece as you?"

Julia kept her voice as calm as possible. "I assure you, most people don't find me in the least prickly. But perhaps your experience of girls isn't quite as comprehensive as you imagine. Some of us are rather choosy, Mr. Galbraith!"

"Touché!" Julia wasn't sure whether he was angry or amused by her words. She didn't care. If she was behaving badly on first acquaintance, then so was he. She had no intention of backtracking.

As it was, his little gesture of understanding had

affected her more than she'd expected it to. And she didn't want to believe there was a gentle heart beating beneath that arrogant exterior. It would destroy her belief in her own first impressions. She searched for something to talk to him about.

"Have you known Aunt Meg long?" At least this was a safe topic of conversation, or so she thought.

"All my life," Vince replied. "She's mentioned you occasionally over the years, but we were beginning to think this Cornish niece couldn't possibly be as perfect as she told us. She was right in one thing, at least. You're very beautiful."

He might have been commenting that the sky was blue for all the emotion in his voice. It was merely a flat statement of fact, and it affronted her as much as his former rudeness, for some reason. It was merely another way of asserting his arrogance when it was said in that offhand way. Julia felt a little shiver run through her. They were standing in a shady part of the garden, and her blouse was thin enough that she could feel the tips of her breasts tauten against the material. It was obvious that Vince was aware of them, too.

"Do you make a habit of disconcerting strangers in this way?" she said in a brittle voice. "I'd heard that Scotsmen were dour, but I'd no idea a compliment could sound so meaningless!"

She saw Vince's eyes glitter. "Oddly enough, I don't get the impression that you and I are strangers anymore, Julia."

His voice softened imperceptibly, and she knew instantly that in any other circumstances that treacherous little lowering of his voice could have the power to send any woman's resistance tumbling . . . any woman but her, she amended silently. She moved away from his penetrating gaze, but her heels had caught fast in the soft ground and she swayed on her feet. If Vince hadn't reached out to steady her she would have fallen. She felt her heart thud as she was held in the circle of his arms.

"Well, you don't have to throw yourself at me, Julia!" He was grinning down at her now.

"I'm never likely to do that—"

Vince's dark eyes were unfathomable and very close to hers. "No? I'm inclined to take that as a challenge, and a Galbraith can never resist a challenge."

He suddenly leaned toward her and touched his mouth to her lips. It was only a fleeting, mocking kiss, done on the spur of the moment, but Julia wrenched away from him. If it wouldn't have seemed like the reaction of a Victorian maiden, she'd have scrubbed her hands across her mouth to wipe away the taste of his lips. It was obvious that it had meant less than nothing to Vince because he had released her from his arms now and caught her by the hand.

"If you can manage to extricate yourself from the mud, we'd better get out of the shade and into the sun before you completely ice up on me. And it's time you saw our spectacular view of Loch Lomond. When you see it, you can tell me then if you've really got a heart as stony as your reactions imply!" Despite the curtness in his manner, he couldn't quite resist the seductive little note creeping into his voice now.

His comment about not being able to resist a challenge was probably all too real, Julia thought instantly. And she'd unwittingly played right into his hands with her coldness. A man like Vince Galbraith would naturally assume it was all an act, and that no girl could resist his charms for long. He held her hand so tightly now she had no chance of breaking free. She refused to respond to him and just let it lie in his palm as if she was quite unaware of it. But she was *very* aware of him. And of the touch of his mouth on hers in that butterfly-soft kiss.

In a way it had been more sensual than a brutal embrace, and it was also the first time any man had kissed her since Martin. And despite all her determination to keep their love sacred and her feelings for Martin intact, Vince Galbraith had managed to storm through her defences as if they were nothing, without even realising it. He'd shattered her glass wall as if it was made of rice paper, and she hated him for it.

Minutes later, she stood on the hillside looking down at the vast, breathtakingly beautiful loch. No amount of description could do it justice as it shimmered in the morning sunlight, its crystal blue waters dotted with islands that resembled green jewels. The loch was pear-shaped, with the widest part of it nearest them, and boats cruising lazily along its length or bobbing gently at its shores. The hills that bordered it on the southern side were soft and green, while in the distance the dark wooded mountains rose dramatically to be lost in the blue-grey mist.

Julia caught her breath at the sheer beauty of it, forgetting for a moment that it was Vince Galbraith who held her hand as her fingers involuntarily tightened and her throat constricted. At times like this she wished she were an artist to capture the beauty spread out below her . . . or a poet who would know the right words. . . . As it was, she could only stand and stare, savouring a moment in time that could never come again. . . .

"I knew just what to expect from your face." His voice was still seductively soft and warm in her ear. "It's like watching a woman in love for the first time."

She couldn't look at him, sensing that his words meant far more than they said. She knew she looked more vulnerable right now than she ever wanted a man to see her, except for the one special man in her life. No man ever had seen her like that except

Martin, and now Vince had snatched even that away from her without even knowing it. Julia wasn't the weepy sort, but right now her eyes were blurred as she sought to keep Martin's memory bright and untarnished in her mind. Somehow the images were misty and his face unclear, and that was one more reason why she hated Vince Galbraith.

By the end of the afternoon Julia began to feel at home with the layout of Galbraith Hall, though she'd still need a guide-map to get her through the maze of corridors. After lunch she and her aunt had been shown their rooms and left to themselves for an hour. They were on different floors, and Julia's room looked out over the loch, to her delight. There was a small balcony outside the tall windows and when she stepped on to it she leaned over the iron railings to take in the glorious sweep of scenery below. The Hall had a small wood to the left of the house, and formal gardens that sloped away down the hillside.

"Impressive, isn't it?" the voice she now knew so well said.

She looked sharply to her right. A little way along there was a balcony identical to hers, on which Vince was seated at a small table, some papers spread out in front of him. "I often work up here in preference to the study, though in summer it's tempting just to sit and look at the scenery instead."

Julia pursed her lips. Whatever "work" he referred to could probably be picked up and dropped whenever he chose, and she guessed that scenery-watching often took priority. Though to be fair, she'd take him more for a doer than a watcher. He was no dreamer, content to let the world pass him by while he remained an onlooker. She was irritated by the way these swift snippets of character analysis kept occurring in regard to Vince Galbraith. She looked away from him toward the shimmer of the loch.

"It's very nice," she said coolly, and Vince burst out laughing.

"And I thought we Northerners were supposed to be guilty of understatement! Anyone who can look out there and say it's merely 'very nice' must be in need of glasses. It's breathtaking!"

It was the word she'd used herself when she'd first seen it, but she wasn't going to admit it to him. She'd never felt so antagonistic toward anyone as she did to Vince Galbraith, not the least because he had raked up old feelings she wanted to share with no one but Martin.

"If you'll excuse me, please, I'm going to have a long soak in the bath before the dinner party tonight."

"I wouldn't dream of keeping you," he said coolly in return.

Julia bristled. Perversely, she made no move to hurry back inside. She leaned against the balcony railings, knowing she'd be framed to advantage against the backdrop of the blue loch and blue-smoke hills. And she was irritated with herself to know she wanted him to look at her, to *see* her framed so beautifully. . . .

"You're not married, I take it?" Her tone implied that no woman would be foolish enough to marry him.

"Are you applying for the post?"

"Of course not," Julia said angrily. He had the uncanny knack of turning everything she said to his own advantage.

"Are you? I don't see any rings on your fingers," he said now.

His voice said it wasn't of the least importance to him, but Julia's face filled with painful colour. She should never have started this kind of question-and-answer game. He was seeing her now all right, she realised, as his eyes flickered with a new interest at her embarrassment. She moved away from the railings.

"No, I'm not," she said shortly.

"I thought not. You have that untouched look about you. It suits some people." His smooth voice didn't let on whether he thought she was one of them. "But please don't let me keep you any longer. Just give me a shout if there's anything you need, Julia—anything at all."

She marched inside as that seductive little note crept into his voice again. He was impossible. She closed the French windows firmly behind her, gathered up her toilet things and the silk robe with the brilliant Chinese design printed on its cool fabric, and went into her bathroom, locking the door with a gesture that was almost childish.

But that was just how he made her feel. For two strangers they certainly struck sparks off each other. Julia also realised slowly that she hadn't felt so alive in months, not since she'd decided once and for all that it was too painful ever to fall in love again.

Not that anything Vince Galbraith stirred up in her could be called love! That certainly wasn't the kind of emotion he generated in her so readily. The odd thing was that he had managed to stir up any kind of emotion at all when she had thought her heart was still numb.

Julia turned on the taps in the bath and sprinkled some bath essence into the warm water. Clouds of perfume rose into her nostrils as she slid the robe from her shoulders and stepped into the water. She lay back in its caressing softness and let the tensions drift away from her. She closed her eyes. . . . Martin had given her the bath essence and whenever she used it she thought of him. It had an intimate, sensuous perfume. For an instant his image was very near, his hands warm and sensitive on her skin, his lips eager and boyishly demanding. . . . Julia's eyes were suddenly moist. They would have grown together . . . and if it hadn't been so perfect, there wouldn't now be this sweet, unfulfilled ache inside her, this longing for his arms and his touch. . . .

The sudden banging of a door in the room next to hers made Julia's eyes open at once. She could hear soft padding footsteps from Vince's room, and the muffled sounds of his voice as he spoke to someone, presumably on the phone. She couldn't hear the words, but the fact that he was so near jarred on her senses, as if he could see, right through the walls, every little intimate movement she made. She finished her bath more hurriedly than she had intended, dried herself in the big fluffy bath towel, slid back into the Chinese robe and lay down on her bed for a short while to cool off.

Rose had said the children would be back from school around four-thirty, and then there'd be a very light tea before they dressed for dinner that evening. Country houses and their occupants seemed to be obsessed with mealtimes, Julia thought sleepily. Though a cup of tea would be very nice right now. . . .

A few minutes later there was a tap on her door. It would be Aunt Meg, coming to ask what she thought of Vince Galbraith and the house. She hardly noticed that his name came to her mind before anything else.

He stood outside her door when she opened it. He still wore the black shirt, though it was opened nearly to the waist now, and the light-coloured slacks that fitted him like a second skin. He held a small silver tray on which there were two glasses and a bottle of white wine.

"I thought we'd call a truce," he said coolly. His eyes took in the soft silkiness of the Chinese robe that caressed her figure. She was sure he knew perfectly well she wore nothing underneath it, and her face flamed with telltale colour as his lips parted in a smile.

"Are we at war?" she countered, trying to sound unconcerned. She could feel the clamminess of her hands. She was furious with herself for appearing so gauche and unworldly, but she hadn't asked for a *tête-à-tête* with him in her room.

"Just the opposite, I hope." The smile was still on his face. "Can I come in, or are we going to stand here and drink in the corridor?"

Where on earth was Aunt Meg, she thought desperately. Why didn't she come and rescue her? At the thought, Julia's nerve came back to her. What on earth was wrong with her, anyway? She wasn't usually put into a state of panic because a dishy young man with an aggressive manner wanted to share a bottle of wine with her. She opened the door defiantly. "Shall we take it on to the balcony?"

In this pink and white bedroom, she was all too aware of him and didn't want to be. . . .

"Don't you think you'll catch cold out there?"

Julia realised he was looking appreciatively at the Chinese robe that had fallen open at the neckline when she held the door wide. It revealed the creamy swellings of her breasts, and she almost snatched at the tie belt and pulled it into a double knot around her slim waist. Vince's eyes sparkled in amusement.

"I'll join you in a minute," she snapped and, grabbing the blue T-shirt and slacks she'd put ready on the bed, fled back to the bathroom and put them on with shaking hands.

Blast the man, she thought angrily. He was spoiling her much-needed holiday with Aunt Meg by stirring up emotions she wanted safely buried. She wondered briefly if this trip had been such a good idea. She'd needed to get away, but she also needed to work. Living the life of the idle rich, like these people, wasn't for her. Too much time on her hands meant too much thinking, and that led to depression. . . .

She disliked Vince Galbraith intensely. Ever since she'd met him the conversation between them had been overwhelmingly personal, and usually to her embarrassment. He had no civilised qualities about him at all. He was pure animal . . . though perhaps those weren't the most apt words to use together. Some women might find him exciting . . . she pushed down the unbidden little thrill at the sudden recollection of being in his arms, and that brief kiss. . . .

Julia joined him on the balcony as he poured two glasses of wine and handed one to her. "To our future, Julia. May it always be as interesting as its beginning."

"As I remember it, our first meeting was a scratchy one when you thought I was about to drop the Ravenscroft piece, and the future you mention will be yours—and mine—not *ours!*" She stressed the word to emphasis her meaning.

"All right. To yours and mine." His eyes teased her. "I like my girls with spirit. Didn't I tell you that?"

She knew he watched to see the effect his use of the plural would have on her, and she tried not to let her soft red lips purse up. Of course she intrigued him, she thought . . . maybe even excited him a little. So she acted like a little ice-maiden . . . his type would try every means in his power to melt the ice if she read him correctly.

The wine was making Julia dizzy. She'd gulped it down nervously, but normally she hardly drank at all. This whole situation was suddenly unreal, and she found herself talking much too fast.

"This is ridiculous." She gave a small giggle. "If anyone had told me a week ago that I'd be standing on a bedroom balcony drinking wine in the afternoon with a man I hardly know, I'd have said they were crazy!"

"What's so wrong about the afternoon?"

Julia giggled again. Oh, no, this was awful, when she was trying to appear cool and sophisticated. Then she saw Vince's eyes darken angrily. As if he thought she was laughing at *him*. She wasn't, for goodness' sake. . . .

"It's just that it seems so—so decadent, if you like. Not quite what 'nice girls do,' or so my old auntie used to tell me," Julia spoke with sudden nervousness.

"Meggie was never that naïve," Vince said shortly. "And most men have got no patience with girls who dress to provoke them and then act the innocent when they get scared."

Julia stared at him, aware that all the tension was back between them again, more brittle than ever.

"Are you talking about me?" she said incredulously.

When had she provoked him? Leaning against the railing of the balcony—well, maybe just a little. But she hadn't asked him to come to her room when she was dressed only in the Chinese robe. She hadn't asked him to kiss her . . . some little devil inside her made her put her glass down as she moved closer to him. What if she *did* tease him a little . . . ? Did the arrogant Vince Galbraith respond like any normal man? The thought flitted through her mind. The soft perfume of her bath essence drifted up between them. She knew darned well she was playing with fire as she looked up into his eyes with a wide-eyed smile, just to test his reactions. . . .

The next minute she was being pulled roughly into his arms, and this time it was more than a fleeting kiss that he pressed on her lips. He bruised her mouth with his own as his arms crushed her tight. The texture of his skin against her own was slightly prickly. She registered it with an unconscious little shock of pleasure. She was unable to protest as Vince kissed her with a bruising passion. For a few seconds, she drowned in its sweet sensuality like a desert thirsty for rain. She'd asked for this and she knew it. Vince Galbraith wasn't a man to take teasing lightly. . . . She felt him move his lips against hers and it was the sexiest thing she had experienced in a long time. Then she felt his hand, warm against the flesh of her midriff in an experimental circling of her skin. . . . Suddenly, she pushed against him with all her strength.

"Stop it," she gasped out. "What on earth do you think you're doing?"

He let her go. He was breathing harshly, but his eyes were hard as he turned from her, downing his drink in one swallow. "I thought you knew very well what I was doing," he said curtly. "Wasn't that what you wanted? You were giving me the great come-on."

"I certainly was not," she said furiously.

She saw the way he looked her over contemptuously. She wouldn't admit to herself he'd aroused a fire in her veins, and she hoped desperately he wasn't aware of it. She hated herself for responding so automatically, and she hated him for arousing her so blatantly. Her feelings showed on her face, and to Vince it was a slight to his masculine pride.

"The permissive society has got a lot to answer for." He was deliberately insulting now. "You all want sexual freedom, but you don't know what to do with it when you've got it."

Julia gasped again. "I never asked to come here." Her voice shook in her rage. "And I certainly wish I hadn't."

"So do I," he retorted. He took his bottle and the glasses and stormed out of her room, banging the door behind him.

Julia stared at it for a long time after he'd gone.

38

This was terrible. She wasn't sure how it had really started, but she and Vince Galbraith had just had a blazing row, and this evening they both had to sit round the dinner table and behave as two civilised people who'd only met that day.

That day! She felt as if she'd always known him. In some ways she felt she knew him better than she'd ever known anyone, even Martin.

The shock of her own thoughts made her clench her hands tightly. She tried desperately to conjure up Martin's face and failed. Instead, she kept seeing that sensual mouth that could be alternately so tender and so cruel . . . the mouth that could excite her with a passion she didn't want when it was pressed on her own . . . seeing those dark, hazel-flecked eyes that could darken even more with anger or desire . . . feeling the touch of his hands and the hardness of his body moulding itself to hers. . . .

"No . . . oh, no . . ." She gave a little moan.

She'd vowed to keep their love intact. She didn't want another man's love to replace the delirious joy she'd known with Martin. But even as she tried to will Martin near to her, some devil inside told her that while Martin's love had been the sweet, wonderful love of an eager boy, Vince's love would be very different. And having known one kind, she was woman enough to appreciate the difference. . . .

"He thinks he's God's gift to women," she snapped aloud. "A man like that would expect to dominate a woman. I bet he'd have a job being faithful to just one, as well, and I could never settle for that. Besides, who believes in love at first sight these days? It's not to be trusted—everyone knows that. . . ."

She stared at her reflection in the bedroom mirror, still fuzzy with wine, her soft cheeks flushed with a fever that was of another kind, her mouth still moist and parted, the touch of Vince's kiss still lingering. What on earth was she going on like this for . . . ?

Love at first sight? Not with a man like that . . . he'd accused her of being a tease, and probably thought she was man-hungry. The thought demoralised her. In future, she'd be very cool when the arrogant Vince Galbraith was around, she thought stoically.

She'd just finished sluicing cold water over her burning cheeks and cooled down a little when Aunt Meg came looking for her to ask what she thought of Rose's treasures. Did that include Vince, Julia thought caustically?

"Oh, there are some wonderful pieces." At least she could be honest about the antiques. "I could spend a week browsing in one room, and I haven't even got round to the books and paintings yet!"

Aunt Meg laughed, having known that Julia's enthusiasm would be stirred at Galbraith Hall.

"I met Vince just now, and he was terribly interested when I mentioned your job to him, Julia. He said he should have guessed you were an expert when you referred to the Ravenscroft piece instead of just the 'pretty glass dish.' I'm sure he'll want to know more about your work later on. He's preparing a historical record of the Hall, you know. Rose has been telling me about it while you had your bath."

"Really?" So he did do something other than swan about the place.

"Some of the pieces are really old, and were brought as gifts by notable people." Aunt Meg didn't notice her sarcasm. "Vince is trying to link them all up so that it's a work of partly biographical detail as well as a straightforward history of the place. The life of Galbraith Hall as told through its antiques, you could say!"

Julia had to admit it sounded interesting.

"Are you coming down to meet the children?"

They were hardly children, Julia discovered when they went down to the drawing room. James was tall and gangling, a younger version of Vince, with the same dark hair and eyes and a ready smile. Fern had a dainty, budding figure and a pertness about her that was almost precocious. She would have been prettier without the sullen look about her mouth. They both had pronounced Scottish burrs to their voices, and the maturity in their eyes that Aunt Meg had told her to expect.

Vince joined them a little later, and Fern turned her attention to him at once. He hardly looked at Julia. He wasn't used to having his advances rejected, she thought bitingly.

"Is Isla coming tonight?" Fern asked impatiently.

"Naturally," Vince replied, smiling.

"Good. Rose says I can have a new outfit for the Games, and I want to ask Isla to get it done for me." Her voice was imperious.

"Isla Macleod owns a tartan shop in Glasgow," Rose told Julia. "Her brother makes wonderful silver jewellery, and they have quite a thriving business between them."

"When Isla and Vince get married, I'm going to be a bridesmaid." Fern preened herself.

"You'll have to wait a long time then." Vince grinned at her.

Julia felt her heart thump. This Isla Macleod must mean something special to him for Fern to talk that way. If they weren't already engaged, they must have an understanding between them, at least. He didn't exactly deny it, anyway. And why should she care? It was nothing to her.

"Just you stop that nonsense, Fern," Rose told her daughter. "Vince will get married in his own good time and not before."

"Isla says I can be a partner in her shop when I'm her sister-in-law." Fern was still wheedling on.

Vince began to laugh. "If you think I'm marrying Isla for you to end up as a shopgirl, you can think again, lassie! You aren't getting an expensive education so you can spend your days selling tartans to tourists!"

"It's good enough for Isla—"

"It's Isla's *business*—"

Rose intervened. "In case you two are going to argue all day, I'll remind you that we have guests in the house. You'll have to forgive Fern's exuberance, Julia. She has a vivid imagination, and her one ambition at the moment is to be like Isla, who you'll have guessed is her idol. You'll meet her later, of course."

Julia was beginning to wish she'd never heard of Isla Macleod. She hadn't missed the little dart of dislike Fern had given her at being snubbed on Julia's account, nor the mocking glance Vince had thrown her way just to see her reaction to Fern's comments about his marriage plans. Whether they were imaginary on Fern's part or not, he needn't think she was in the least interested, Julia thought. Maybe he really was serious about this Isla Macleod, or maybe she was just one of a string of girls. Julia had no intention of being another.

Chapter Three

"What are the Games?" she asked, mainly to get her thoughts away from the topic of Vince's love life.

"It's a charity event we always support." It was Fern who answered carelessly. "Vince presents some of the prizes and Rose acts like queen for the day. It's quite good fun, really," she added quickly, as her mother gave her a quelling look. "I'm taking part in the dancing this year."

"You and Meg must join us, Julia. It's always held in a little highland village that suddenly bursts at the seams for the day when the tourists swarm in."

"Thank you," she said dutifully to Rose. It sounded interesting, but she didn't really want to be swept up in the Galbraith entourage any more than she had to. She caught the scowl on Fern's face at Rose's invitation, and thought she could do without too much of the girl's old/young image. James was quieter than his sister, and less volatile. Aunt Meg had told Julia he was a clever lad who would go on to university eventually. Until her sudden desire to work with Isla, Fern had wanted to go to a finishing school in Switzerland, Aunt Meg had confided. No doubt, her ambition would change many times again, the way adolescent ideas often did.

As soon as the little tea party was over, Julia went

to her room to start getting ready for the dinner party. It was suddenly important for her to look her best, even if it meant seeing the insolent appraisal in Vince's eyes again. She felt the slow thudding of her heart, and the pulse beat in her throat, as she remembered it. Oh, yes, she thought weakly, there was a fire in him that touched an answering spark in her, whether she wanted it or not. And a spark could easily become a flame . . . such men had the devil's touch when it came to women. And Vince Galbraith was undeniably sensual and charismatic, but any woman who gave in to him would be like a leaf in the wind to his desires.

No other man had had such an instant effect on her, Julia realised shakily. Her love for Martin had grown slowly, and even that had held nothing like the surge of emotion Vince aroused in her. It wasn't *love,* she insisted to herself again. The feelings he evoked in her were far more basic than that. . . . She closed her eyes for a brief moment. She didn't want to imagine what it would be like to lie in his arms, but the image of it seemed to envelop and crush her, the way his embrace had done earlier, sending wild, sweet sensations coursing through her. . . . She had to thrust him out of her mind with a deliberate effort.

Later, she walked slowly down the wide carpeted staircase at Galbraith Hall in her slender-heeled silver shoes, the cool black silk of her dress caressing her soft curves. Her shoulders were smoothly golden and bare, the neckline of the dress low enough to draw the eye, but still not too provocative. She wore a single gold chain round her neck and small gold earrings. Her makeup was subtle and perfect, the glorious chestnut hair pinned on top of her head with long soft tendrils giving her a deceptively fragile look. Over her arm was draped her gossamer silvery shawl. She looked stunning, and the eyes of several male guests told her so.

Almost immediately, she was introduced to a tall, good-looking man with friendly grey eyes and a shock of light brown hair. This was Andrew Macleod, brother of Isla, who fashioned silver jewellery. He had an easy, bantering manner, and Julia liked him at once.

"Come and meet my sister," Andrew said a little later when half a dozen names had gone through her head. She'd never remember them all. But she'd remember the cool and elegant Isla Macleod. . . .

Her hair was ash-blond, worn in a shining cap that framed her face perfectly. She wore a slender cocktail dress of flame-coloured silk with a knee-high split at one side that revealed a long shapely leg every time she moved. The dress clung seductively to her superb figure, and in the deep vee of her neckline was an intricate piece of silver jewellery that Julia learned later was Andrew's work. Isla looked Julia up and down and dismissed her as a rival, if Julia interpreted the glance correctly.

"So you're the little niece I've been hearing about, are you?" Isla's mouth smiled, but her words were meant to be demoralising.

"And you're the owner of the tartan shop in Glasgow." Julia smiled back. She'd nearly said "the shopkeeper," but one of them being coolly insulting was enough.

"And how do you like our highlands, Julia? I'm sure you have nothing like them in Cornwall. I went there on a very short holiday years ago, but I was glad to get away. Nasty sea-mists and hordes of tourists everywhere, as I recall it."

Julia kept the smile fixed on her face. "Oh, it has a quaint, rustic charm for people who find too much sophistication boring," she said lightly, unable to resist the barb.

"Really? I never found it so. Too much rustication rubs one the wrong way, doesn't it?" She turned away as Vince joined their little group, and instantly her chiselled beauty became vibrantly alive. And Julia herself forgot the other girl's nastiness as her heart gave a great leap at the sight of Vince.

He was magnificent in a swirling kilt and dazzling white-frilled shirt, with a black velvet jacket and bow tie. She'd never seen a man in full Highland dress until now, and if anyone had ever put the idea in motion that it was unmanly, it was completely dispelled by the sight of Vince Galbraith. All the other men wore dinner suits, elegant and correct, but Vince . . . Vince was a man to the nth degree . . . electrifying. . . .

As Julia watched, Isla immediately put her arm possessively through Vince's, and the "Keep Off" signs were loud and clear. Julia didn't object when Andrew called her over to introduce her to more of the guests. Suddenly, she found the sight of Isla and Vince together almost too much.

But once the guests assembled in the dining room, she discovered that though she was seated next to Andrew, Vince was directly opposite her, and Isla next to him. Julia let her eyes admire the beautiful room rather than dwell on that fact. It was a lovely room, with a beautiful rosewood table dominating it, and side tables all the way round. Above the main table was a magnificent crystal chandelier, but to-night the occasion was graced by the flattering lights of tall candles. The old Galbraith silver gleamed as brilliantly as shimmering jewels and sparkling eyes. And Julia's eyes were finally drawn inevitably to those directly opposite her.

Vince lifted his glass to her, reminding her instant-ly of when he'd done the same thing on her balcony. Julia flushed slightly, remembering too the crushing embrace that had followed, perfectly aware that Isla didn't miss one little bit of the mute exchange between them.

She needn't worry, Julia thought swiftly. Vince hadn't even told her she looked lovely, though she'd half expected it. Perversely, she was annoyed that he hadn't. But, glancing at him across the table from time to time, she knew he was telling her constantly, with his eyes, his mouth, with every pore of him.

"How long are you staying in Scotland, Julia?" The question from Isla was interested, but her eyes were hard.

"I haven't decided yet." Julia's reply was just as cool.

"I certainly hope you'll stay awhile," Andrew said. "Will you come out with me one evening, Julia? You know that dining at the same table establishes something special between two people, don't you?"

"Does it?" She laughed into his nice grey eyes.

Then it also established something between her and Vince, she supposed. Unwillingly, she found her eyes drawn to his through the haze of the candle-light.

"I've got a proposition to make to you, Julia," Vince said suddenly. "I gather Meggie's already told you about the historical record I'm working on. It's going pretty slowly, but it would be a lot easier if I had somebody to assist me who knew something about antiques. I need them catalogued and proper-ly dated, and as you're 'between jobs' at the moment —how about it? What do you say to moving in here to give poor Meggie room to breathe again, and working for me?"

His eyes challenged her. She heard Aunt Meg protesting down the table that he might have put it more subtly than that or Julia would think she didn't want her to stay. She saw Fern's scowl, and knew instinctively that that little madam didn't want any-body else around to take Vince's attention from Isla, whom she clearly saw as some kind of glamourous goddess. She saw Isla's furious flash of jealousy before she covered it with a sugary smile. . . .

Julia knew she should refuse. That, whatever

Vince said, he didn't really need an assistant. Yes, it would make the work much easier and quicker, but he'd managed perfectly well on his own so far. She knew she'd be playing with fire to accept. Nor did she need to move in, did she . . . ? But Aunt Meg needed her car and there was no bus service that could get her here . . . and hadn't she already decided that she *needed* to work . . . ? She was weakening by the minute.

She met Vince's challenging eyes again. *I dare you,* they said to her. Thoughts whirled round in her brain, seeming to take an eternity, but in reality it was only seconds. *I dare you,* his eyes said. . . .

"All right." Julia's voice was suddenly breathless, as if she'd been running. "If the job's open, I accept—if you're sure you want me. I can get references, if you like."

His smile widened at her hurried afterthought. He'd already made it blatantly obvious that he wanted her. . . .

"References won't be necessary." His voice was oddly expressionless, yet something about it made her shiver. "I'll take you just the way you are."

Isla's furious face told Julia she was perfectly aware of the double meaning such a remark could hold. She turned to Julia, her eyes barely concealing the malice she felt.

"So you're interested in antiques, are you?" Her tone said it was probably what one might expect from a girl from the sticks who was out of touch with contemporary life.

"I've worked with them for some time," Julia replied coolly. "It probably sounds deadly dull to other people, but there's enormous excitement and satisfaction in discovering a treasure that has been dust-laden for years, or being able to match a piece to its twin and realise its value has increased ten-fold—"

"Good Lord!" Isla was looking at her now with condescending amusement as Julia couldn't stop her enthusiasm showing through. "I can think of better things to get excited about than a load of old junk!"

"You would, darling," Vince said lazily.

Isla instantly turned on a dazzling smile for his benefit. "Well, nobody could call any of your lovely old things junk, Vince, and you know very well I wasn't referring to any of them! But I couldn't go grubbing about in somebody's old attic in dusty old clothes if I was paid a fortune." She intimated that anyone who did was crazy.

"And I don't think I could spend all day behind the counter in a shop!" The words were out before Julia could stop them. She wasn't normally catty, but she knew that this woman would always bring out the worst in her. And it irritated her still more to realise that Vince was well aware of the rivalry between them and was enjoying it. Just as if he thought he was the cause of it, Julia thought scathingly, choosing to ignore the fact that he was perfectly right. . . .

Later she discovered that Isla had her own clever little warfare tactics. When the party retired to the drawing room again and Isla was surrounded by her own little clique of young people, she would turn time and again to Julia in mock dismay.

"Julia, dear, it's unforgivable of us to shut you out. You must come and join in, mustn't she, Vince? I was just telling them all, Julia . . ."

She would go on to relate some tale they had all heard before while Julia listened in embarrassment and anger. The "game" established Isla and Vince as a couple, and placed Julia very much in the position of outsider. It was cleverly done, and Isla's eyes flashed the message at her time and again. "This is my territory" they said. . . .

"Oh, we've heard all that before, Isla," Fern

grumbled from time to time as the patient voice trilled on as if she were explaining things to a child. And Isla would turn to her with reproach in her lovely eyes.

"Fern, Julia's a stranger in our midst! Give her a chance to follow our accents and do stop being so impatient. You and I have all the time in the world to chatter!"

In other words, Julia was a slow-witted simpleton, the cool voice implied, and she and this sister of the man she intended to marry were as thick as thieves. Julia was more than thankful when there was a sudden clamouring for James to do his party-piece and tell the story of the Galbraith ghost, insisting that the usual ritual should be followed since there was a new listener among them.

At that point everyone sat in a semicircle on the expensive silk cushions that were scattered on the deep-pile carpet in the drawing room for that purpose. The lights were put out, and only a couple of tall candles were left burning. And James, once coaxed into telling his tale, put more expression into it than Julia would have expected.

The story was a predictable one . . . a lovelorn Scottish lad far below the social standing of the clannish Galbraiths who wooed away a beautiful ancestor of Vince's and fled across the border with her to England, from where they were never seen again. The signal for their flight was the plaintive sound of the pipes, at which the lad had great skill, and a certain lament seemed to symbolise the tragedy of their love.

If tragedy it was . . . for at least the lovers were together, and escaped the wrath of the fierce Galbraiths of that time, but the fact still remained that the lad was said to pine for his native Scotland. And on still nights one could sometimes hear the sound of a lone piper playing longingly, as if still calling for his homeland and his love . . . still waiting somewhere beside the tranquil waters of Loch Lomond . . . and that only those in love could hear it. . . .

At that point Julia nearly jumped out of her skin when the unmistakable sound of the bagpipes filtered through the air from somewhere outside the house. A shiver ran through her. She felt her heart pounding, and hardly noticed Fern's stifled giggling, nor the fact that no one else seemed particularly surprised. Seconds later the long silk curtains at the French windows rustled and blew into the room, and somebody turned on the lights as Vince stepped inside, resplendent in his Highland clothes, the bagpipes under his arms filling the air with their bittersweet, poignant music. His eyes were on Julia's face as the room was flooded with light and sound, and she couldn't resist the thought that he'd probably engineered this ghost story for some deep purpose of his own. . . .

"Oh, I'm sorry, Julia," Isla was gasping with mirth at the expression on her face, and Julia jerked away as the Scots girl put a cool hand on her arm. "It's cruel to laugh, but if you could see your face just now . . . !"

Vince had put the bagpipes down to a round of applause. He strode across the room toward Julia, pulled her to her feet and planted a kiss on her lips. From the little cheer that followed, Julia assumed that this was all part of the family ritual, too. Well, let them have their fun, she thought savagely. The buzz of conversation was returning now as the cushions were replaced on the furniture and Vince still held her hands and spoke softly to her.

"You'll have to forgive us quaint Scots our fairy tales, Julia. I assure you that you won't be haunted by the Lovers' Lament tonight—unless you're in love, that is. There's no telling what you might hear then."

* * *

Julia and her aunt were the only house guests at the Hall, and as the next day was Saturday the children were home from their boarding schools for the weekend. To Julia's relief they had already gone out when she got up, and Aunt Meg told her they'd gone boating on Loch Lomond. Rose filled in the details over breakfast.

"Vince has a powerful motorboat, but when they're on their own the children have to be content with rowboats. Isla has a passion for water sports, so she's often there as well, when she can persuade Vince to take her water-skiing. How about you, Julia?"

"Good heavens, no! I can swim, and I used to like messing about with boats in Cornwall, but that's very different from what you're describing." She laughed to cover the sudden memory of herself and Martin hauling a dinghy over a sandy beach and then collapsing in a heap, with the taste of salt on their kisses and the glow of being together making them oblivious to everything else.

She realised with a little shock that she'd hardly thought of Martin since arriving at Galbraith Hall. Not in the way she used to, and the thought filled her with an odd little sense of guilt.

"I hope you haven't changed your mind about working for me since last night." Vince's voice startled her as she helped herself to toast and eggs for breakfast that morning.

She sat down at the dining table and answered him coolly. "Of course not. It sounds fascinating. I just hope you realise what a luxury it will be for me to work among such beautiful things. It won't seem like work at all."

He seated himself opposite her, tanned and casual this morning in easy-fitting roll-necked sweater and jeans, his plate filled with crisp bacon and tomatoes.

"I assure you I can be a slave driver. But, of course, we must get it all on a businesslike footing, and if you'll come to the study after breakfast, Julia, we'll sort out the details, such as salary and work schedule and so on."

He was so formal it was hard to believe he'd forced those ardent kisses on her yesterday, or teased her with a piper's legend when he'd stood so magnificently in the moonlight in his Highland rig-out, the cool rustling of the silk curtains adding to the sudden eeriness of his appearance.

Half an hour later she was sitting on the other side of the beautiful Chippendale desk in the study while Vince outlined his proposed work to her. She felt a growing respect as she listened, realising that this was no idle playboy taking up a fancy to write a book to fill in the time, but a man with a real desire to trace some of his ancestry through the items collect-ed and gifted to the family over the centuries, to write a historical record with a difference, in fact. Whether it would have much commercial value was clearly of little consideration. What mattered to Vince was that Rose and the children and himself should know all there was to know and to have something solid to pass on to future generations.

"Though I sometimes think the rest of them only show an interest because it means a lot to me," he said ruefully. "Rose is still an Englishwoman, de-spite her years in Scotland. Once she sees me safely married, as she likes to put it, I've no doubt she'll be off again on her jaunts round the world, more or less in perpetual motion. The children too . . . well, they've no wish to settle in what they think of as a backwater, so in some ways this is an indulgence for *my* children, if I ever have any!"

The conversation was getting too personal again, and Julia realised she didn't want to pursue the idea of Vince's children, particularly in relation to the only girl she'd met who took such a proprietary interest in him—Isla Macleod.

"I think I've found the right person to be part of my venture," he said softly, sending the warm colour to her cheeks.

Rather than try to guess whether he was reverting to his double-meanings game again, Julia commented that if he wanted her help, he'd better refrain from abusing the antiques! Vince laughed, leaning forward to touch a tendril of her long dark hair as it lay on the nape of her neck.

"Beautiful things were made to be used and enjoyed, weren't they?" The timbre of his voice deepened and she knew instinctively that he was going to kiss her again. She moved back in her chair, pulling away from his fingers. Even if she wanted any kind of flirtation with him . . . any kind of affair . . . he went too fast. He left her breathless . . . afraid. . . .

"You mentioned salary." Her voice was clipped. "Since I assume I won't have to pay for my room and board, I expect you to take that into consideration, of course."

He mentioned a figure that stopped her in midsentence.

"Don't be ridiculous." She was angry with him now. "That's far more than I was getting with Mr. Pollard. . . ."

"But I'm not Mr. Pollard, and I want you more than he did," Vince said calmly. There was a glint of battle in his dark eyes now, and the hazel flecks were very obvious in them. He no longer tried to touch her, but she could still feel the pressure of his fingers on her neck. And his eyes told her what he wanted of her.

"Do you always manage to buy what you want?" she heard herself snap.

"Usually. Most things can be bought if the price is right."

"And people?" Oh, no, this was a fine way to be talking to a new employer, but she couldn't seem to stop herself.

But in one of those mercurial changes of mood she was beginning to know, Vince threw back his dark head and laughed. "All right, we'll leave the salary question open for the moment. Let's just say you won't be underpaid and I shall expect value for money. There may be some travelling to be done and unsocial hours. . . ."

"Travelling?" Julia wasn't so much thrilled at this as suspicious. What kind of travelling was needed for a book of family history?

"Oh, you won't need your passport," Vince said coolly. "But you'll appreciate that there's no problem in tracing the ancestry part of the book. What I need to know about that is all contained in family records and so on. I need more than that, though. It's the various items in the house that I particularly want to tie up with various visits and so on that may need chasing up. I propose going to Aberdeen shortly, where there are some excellent archives for what we need, and they'll be of interest to you, as well, since they deal in the kind of historical memorabilia we shall detail. Then, too, I've exchanged letters with a descendant of an ancient Galbraith groom who has a few relics of interest we might look at. He lives on the Isle of Skye, so a trip over there will be on the agenda. Am I whetting your appetite?"

He knew very well he was. Julia's suspicions disappeared as he spoke, and she knew this job could be an exciting one as well as absorbing. Delving back into history by means of the antiques she loved was just up her alley, and at least it was one thing she and this dynamic man had in common.

Vince suddenly glanced at his watch. "I've some business to attend to this morning, but if you're interested, I'll take you out on the loch this afternoon. If you're not afraid of a high-powered boat, of course. She's pretty fast."

"I'd love it," Julia told him.

"Good, then we'll go after lunch." Vince slid off the desk and held the door open for her. He was an odd mixture of the primitive and the conventional, she thought.

It was crazy, but once he'd gone the morning lost a little of its lustre. It was as if his personality dominated the place, so that it was less of a house without him. Later, her aunt suggested they both stroll round the grounds together.

"Are you happy with the arrangements, love?" Aunt Meg asked her anxiously. "You didn't have to accept, you know, but as soon as Vince heard about your old job he leapt at the chance of getting your assistance. I hope I didn't do the wrong thing in telling him."

"Of course not. It would have come up sooner or later, anyway," Julia assured her. Her innate honesty forced her to admit that she was glad to have a genuine reason for staying on at the Hall, for getting to know Vince better, but at a proper distance, without the assault on her emotions he'd shown her yesterday.

"I'm not moving in here right away, though," she told her aunt firmly. "I came to stay with you, and the Galbraiths will have to wait a week or so until we've finished our holiday properly. It won't hurt Vince not to have it all his own way for once."

Aunt Meg chuckled. "I could see the way the wind was blowing between you two last night! And you're right—he does like to have things going his way. It won't hurt him to meet a girl with a bit of fire in her veins. Most of the ones around here are dazzled by his wealth and charm."

Julia was dying to ask what her aunt thought about Isla, but it might make it obvious that she didn't like the other girl. As if her aunt read her thoughts,

Isla's name cropped up a little later on as they strolled through the formal gardens with the last roses still filling the air with their heady scent.

"If you've a yen to buy any tartan while you're here, we might call in at Isla Macleod's shop in Glasgow one day next week, love. It really is the best for miles, and she'll get anything made up by her own dressmaker very speedily."

"Is that what Fern was talking about then—for these games?" Julia asked.

"That's right. It'll be nice to go in a party—and by then, you'll be part of the Galbraith household anyway! So I'll be quite entitled to come along!" Aunt Meg was teasing, but it gave Julia an odd feeling to realise it was true. She didn't specially want to meet Isla again, but she was curious to see this shop of which she'd heard so much now, and also Andrew's jewellery.

Vince arrived back just before lunch, whisking Julia off in his sleek blue car as soon as they'd finished eating. The children hadn't come back at all, as they'd taken a picnic lunch with them, and Julia felt a stab of disappointment when Vince told her they'd be joining them later. No matter how she tried, she couldn't feel entirely easy in Fern's company, particularly since the girl seemed to resent her so much. No doubt since she was so obsessed with the idea of Vince marrying Isla, she saw every other girl as a potential threat to her ambitions. It was ridiculous, of course. . . .

She forced herself to forget Fern and Isla in the exhilaration of being on the boat with Vince. The boat streaked across the shimmering stretch of water, weaving its way among the islands.

"It's marvellous." She had to shout above the roar of the engine. "It's like being in another world!"

He slowed the speed down so they could talk more easily. "Didn't I tell you? It's certainly put a bloom on your cheeks. You've come alive, Julia!" His mouth was close to her ear, his arm round her waist. Unconsciously, she flinched away from his touch, and he looked at her with a frown between his eyes.

"Sorry. I'd forgotten you were untouchable," he mocked her.

His tone reminded her of Isla at the dinner party, and she shrugged at once. They both tormented her in different ways.

"It depends who's touching me," she retorted. "And before you start asking if I'm a man-hater, no, I'm not."

"I see. It all depends on the man, does it?"

The tension between them flared up again. Julia could hardly believe it had all happened so quickly. They'd been cruising pleasantly only minutes ago, and now they were snapping angrily at each other.

"You could say that," she said edgily.

Vince let the boat bob gently in the water. On the bank, Julia could see Fern and James waving madly, but Vince ignored them for the moment.

"What kind of saint does this incredible man have to be?" he taunted. "I'd be surprised if there's one alive who can match up to your requirements."

Julia felt her face blanch. He didn't realise the accuracy of his remark, of course, but it didn't stop the sudden feeling of emptiness inside her, or the sweet surging memories of Martin.

"There isn't," she said abruptly. She averted her eyes from his belligerent gaze.

There was a moment of silence, broken only by the small swish of water against the bows of the boat.

"I can't decide whether that's meant to be a provocative statement or not," he said finally.

"Then please believe me when I tell you it's not!"

"In other words, you just dislike me—is that it?" He simply wouldn't leave it alone. He was too self-opinionated to believe she could really mean it unless she put it into words. She could sense it in the sheer incredulity in his voice. Julia rounded on him, and his dark good looks so close to her made her heart give that uncomfortable little leap again. Oh, yes, she could like him very much, but she wouldn't give him the satisfaction of feeding his ego.

"Let's just say I'd like you a lot more if you didn't keep trying to make more of our relationship than there is. I'm quite happy to work with you, but that's as far as it goes."

"I see. As long as I toe the line like a good little boy, I suppose. Well, it's not my style, Julia, and I don't care to make promises I can't keep." He didn't hide his annoyance at her coolness; he had obviously expected a different reply to his question.

Suddenly, Vince started up the engine again with a roar and before Julia could protest he had pulled her toward the wheel.

"You wanted to enjoy an afternoon's boating, so that's what we'll do," he said calmly. "Take her in."

"I can't!" Julia gasped.

"You'll be all right if I hold you. I promise not to molest you between here and the bank." He oozed sarcasm now.

He stood very close behind her, his large, capable hands covering hers as she gripped the wheel in momentary terror. But very soon she was able to relax as the knowledge that it was Vince who was really in control seeped into her dizzy mind. He kept his hands tightly over hers as the boat scythed through the water, as close as one person, neither of them solely in control of the boat, part of a team, each needing the other. . . . Julia was very conscious of his strength as he stood tautly behind her. She could feel the powerful muscles in his thighs touching hers; she could hear his heartbeats against her back, feel his breath on her cheek, and the brush of his lips against them. . . . She suddenly caught sight of Fern and James on the bank. James was waving, while Fern stood sullenly, waiting for the boat to slow down and pick them up at the jetty.

Julia felt an uncomfortable lurch of her heart at the unfriendly look in Fern's eyes as she and her brother clambered aboard.

"She really goes, doesn't she?" James yelled at Julia once they were under way again.

"She certainly does." Julia smiled. She'd forgiven him his ghost story last night, and, as always, he was more relaxed now that she wasn't quite such a stranger. Fern stood in the bow of the boat like a hostile figurehead, and finally she strolled back to where Julia was watching the frothy wake in the water behind them.

"Vince is practically engaged to Isla, you know," she stated baldly.

Julia hid a smile. The girl was so obvious in her dislike she couldn't take her seriously. It was a pity, but there it was. They just didn't hit it off. . . .

As if Fern saw the smile as a threat, she spoke furiously, in a low voice so the others couldn't hear. "Well, he won't marry *you,* that's for sure. He and Isla went off for a weekend in the summer and she told me a few things then! My goodness, did she tell me some things! I thought they'd come back engaged, but I daresay she'll want Andrew to make her a special ring for that. It'll not be long now, though, just you see!"

She flounced off to join her brother, while Julia stared after her. She could hardly disbelieve everything she'd just heard, though she was aware that her spirits were zooming down as quickly as they'd soared with the magic of the loch. So what, she tried to ask herself? She hadn't imagined that Vince Galbraith had been a saint before she arrived in his life, but the information that Fern had just told her so spitefully, that Vince and Isla had spent a weekend together in the summer, that was more serious. That wasn't some vague incident in his past that needn't matter a hang to anyone else. Isla was still very much on the scene, and had made it plain to Julia that she regarded Vince as her property.

Now Julia realised it might very well be true. And if that were so, Vince had no right to play around with someone else's emotions the way he had with hers. No right to stir up feelings inside her that she'd kept successfully dormant until now.

Her eyes suddenly stung as the boat roared along the length of the loch and her vision was blurred by the sharp yellow gorse on the hillside nearest to them. The gorse that always reminded her of Martin and the kissing time. . . . Only now when she thought of it, it was another mouth she imagined kissing hers with sudden passion or unexpected tenderness . . . a sensual mouth she knew had the power to disturb her beyond her wildest dreams.

She knew that whatever she felt for Vince Galbraith, it could never be indifference. She was drawn to him despite herself, but even if the desire he felt was ever to develop into something more on his part, she knew she would demand an exclusive love.

And from what she had learned from Fern about his attachment to Isla, it was doubtful whether he even knew the meaning of the words, she thought bitterly.

Chapter Four

Fern spent a lot of time on the phone that evening. When she returned to the drawing room where everyone was relaxing after dinner, she spoke directly to Vince.

"Isla's going to let me have a look through her samples in the morning if you'll take me to the shop, big brother," she said coaxingly. "If I choose what I want, she'll have her dressmaker run it up by next weekend. I said Rose would be sure to ask her back for lunch afterwards, and then maybe we could go to the loch again in the afternoon."

"They should have named you plotter." Vince laughed. "It's all right with me, but you'd better ask Rose about lunch."

"Of course Isla can come to lunch." Rose was coolly agreeable. "Why not invite Andrew, as well. Since Julia won't be going back to Strathrowan with Meg until tomorrow morning, you might as well make it a bit of a party while the weather still holds good."

"Great!" Fern made for the door. "I'll call Isla again and tell her. Andrew won't object, I know. He took a fancy to Julia last night."

Julia didn't miss the darting look Fern had shot her way as she left the room, and knew that the girl had somehow intended things to move exactly the way they had. Though why on earth she should have made that remark about Andrew Macleod fancying her was beyond her, Julia thought in exasperation.

Glancing at Vince's face a minute later, she thought she knew very well. That little madam had decided to stir things up in case her brother was showing too much interest in another girl when it was clear that Fern wanted Isla Macleod for a sister-in-law. And with Rose unintentionally adding to the illusion of herself and Andrew making an extra couple for the following afternoon, Vince's face had assumed the brooding look Julia was coming to know. Why should he even care? He had one female dotty about him, and probably plenty of others, but he was the type who couldn't resist adding another scalp to his belt.

Well, if that was the way he wanted it, she'd show him he wasn't the only pebble on the beach. . . . She was beginning to think in clichés, Julia thought irritably, but she intended giving all her attention to Andrew Macleod on Sunday afternoon, even if it meant a little harmless flirtation. Anything to show this self-assured man scowling into space that not every girl fell immediately under his spell. . . .

Julia went to bed early that night, saying she was tired after the previous evening, which had gone on into the wee small hours. In the pink and white bedroom she undressed and stood at her window with the lights turned off for a long time. Far below the clear waters of Loch Lomond were like a beautiful mirror in the moonlight. It was a lovers' paradise here, she thought with a little catch in her throat, so beautiful and romantic with the little islands like inkblots from this distance, and the smudge of trees and foliage surrounding the loch. Still farther away was the towering blue haze of the mountains as they merged with the sky. . . . There was something magical about the distant mountains and the still clear waters of the loch. Something to catch at your heart as nowhere else, Julia thought. Scotland was an enchanted land of mists and glens and a stormy past, of ancient traditions and royal intrigues, and the pure clean air that was fragrant with the dew-fresh scent of blossoms and heather as she gazed out the window. She could almost imagine those Galbraith lovers clasped in each other's arms in a clandestine meeting, warmed by their love, and bewitched by the perfection around them.

Julia turned abruptly. She didn't want to think of romantic settings that could tear your heart with their beauty, nor of lovers' meetings. For a second, she imagined she could hear the plaintive sound of a piper and her heart gave a little leap, but it was only a bird crying in the night. . . . She was restless, despite the fact that she'd pleaded tiredness downstairs. But she wasn't tired, and all her senses were alive tonight.

She realised that she hadn't taken off the small gold pendant she wore round her neck and put it in the jewel case she always carried with her. There was nothing of great value there, save for one or two antique pieces she'd bought at cost price from Mr. Pollard. But her fingers touched the small square box in which lay her engagement ring, and after a second's hesitation she opened it and drew it out.

It was a heart-shaped ring, studded with tiny diamonds. In a way, it was like Martin himself—boyish, romantic, young. . . . Julia had decided not to wear it anymore after the few weeks following Martin's death. It caused too much comment. People she knew well couldn't seem to avoid glancing at it and then looking away in embarrassment; new acquaintances sometimes asked smilingly when the wedding was going to be. . . . In the end, she had put it away in its little box, feeling in a way that it was a small betrayal of all she and Martin had meant to each other, but unable to be reminded every single day. . . .

For the first time in months, Julia slipped the ring back on her finger. It felt cold and unfamiliar after so long, and slightly loose, reminding her that she had lost a few pounds in recent months. She waited for the glow the ring should have given her, but there was nothing. Without Martin and the meaning behind it, it was just a piece of jewellery, nothing more. She felt the stab of tears in her eyes, knowing she'd been holding on to a dream all this time, and that the dream had been imperceptibly slipping away. She wasn't naïve enough not to realise that hearts did mend, and that in time she might even be ready to form at least a warm friendship with another man, even though she still shied away from the idea of love, but she hadn't expected it to happen yet . . . not so soon. . . . She still needed to hold on to the special, misty enchantment of first love that had been hers and Martin's.

Julia replaced the ring in its box and closed the lid. The lump in her throat was for things past that would never come again: a phone call to make her heart sing, a birthday card that was all sentiment and roses, a menu from the restaurant where Martin had asked her to marry him. What was the use of looking back, a small voice whispered inside her? Life goes on, and life is for living. Martin, of all people, would have echoed the well-worn phrases, and she knew it. And whether she liked it or not, it was happening to her.

Next morning she told Aunt Meg she wanted to explore on her own, knowing she and Rose would be happy enough by themselves. James was off on his own pursuits, and Vince now was committed to taking Fern into Glasgow, so she knew there'd be no unwelcome attentions from him. All the same, she felt a little pang when she heard the blue car roar off down the lane as she climbed the hillside in her jeans and long boots, a sweater tied loosely round her neck over her thin shirt in case the weather got suddenly cooler. She had tied her long hair back behind her head in a pony tail, and Aunt Meg commented that she looked as young as Fern as she set off. And twice as vulnerable, Julia thought ruefully, guessing that that young lady could take care of herself pretty well.

She hadn't realised that climbing to the top of the hill behind Galbraith Hall would give such unexpected and spectacular views. She could see where the Firth of Clyde stretched out into the ocean, the Isle of Bute guarding its entrance. Beyond, the misty mass of the Isle of Arran loomed out of the blue water, green-grey and mysterious. Nearer, directly below, the river Clyde forked in two directions. All around were green fertile hills and sparkling blue waters. A lone hiker in highland garb nodded good-morning and strode on, stout stick in hand, good Scottish walking boots on his feet. Julia felt a sudden urge to laugh out loud from sheer happiness. Cornwall and its associations were another world, and suddenly she knew this was the world she wanted. This was home, as if all the ancestors she'd never known were welcoming her back as a true daughter of Scotland. Fanciful it might be, but it was a feeling that put a glow in her heart.

She was rosy-cheeked by the time she returned to Galbraith Hall, but it had been a sparkling morning and the fresh air and her strange revelation had restored her as always. The blue car was already there in the drive, together with another sleek little job in acid yellow. Very suitable for Isla, Julia thought with a smile.

Fern glimpsed her in the corridor and called her in to show her the samples of material she'd chosen. Such friendliness could only be for a purpose, Julia guessed, and when she saw Isla, ultracool in white slacks and black sweater, she knew the reason for it. At once she felt all hands and feet, the typical country girl, in fact, and Isla's amused smile told her she too appreciated the difference in their appearances. Vince was nowhere to be seen, but Andrew was there, saying he was glad to see her again. She admired the tartan for Fern's new kilt for the dancing, the fine white silk for the blouse which was to be ruffled and flounced, and the sleek black velvet for the bodice. All to be made up in extra quick time. When the Galbraiths wanted a job done, they got it done!

"If you'll excuse me, I'll change before lunch," Julia said quickly. She felt at a distinct disadvantage compared with Isla right now. As she turned, she cannoned straight into Vince, who caught her in his arms.

"I do believe the ice-maiden's beginning to melt." His voice was half-teasing as he spoke so that only she could hear, but she knew he hadn't really forgiven her for her affront to his masculinity yesterday. She felt even more gauche as she extricated herself from his arms, her heart banging in her chest at the sudden encounter.

"Don't tease the poor girl, Vince." Isla hadn't heard the words, but her sweet voice told Julia she didn't like private little moments between another woman and Vince. Isla's manicured hand was on his arm possessively. "Anyone can see she's not used to your brand of high-powered chatting-up."

"Thanks, Isla, but I wasn't born yesterday," Julia was stung into replying.

"You look it, dear . . . oh, I meant that as a compliment, of course! You look as young and pretty as Fern with that cute little ponytail, doesn't she, Vince?" The voice was still sugary.

Julia seethed as he looked her up and down. His eyes were unsmiling, his gaze insolently personal. She couldn't be sure whether he enjoyed the little set-to between herself and Isla or not, but he could hardly be unaware of it.

"Oh, she's more than pretty," he answered lightly. "She'd do justice to one of those 'natural look' holiday posters."

"When you've both finished discussing me, I'd like to pass," she said tightly, as Vince still barred her way. He laughed at her red-faced reaction to his remark.

"Oh, let her go, darling." Isla was becoming irritated now. "You'll have her bursting into tears with embarrassment in a minute. And she'll end up believing every word you say, and that would be fatal."

Andrew suddenly appeared in the room to catch Isla's last remarks. "Take no notice of them, Julia," he summed up the situation. "I can guess how they've been baiting you. They're old hands at the game, but it's best to ignore them." He grinned to take the sting out of his words.

And that just about underlined the fact that Vince and Isla had a perfect understanding between them, Julia thought bitingly. She slid under Vince's arm and went upstairs with as much dignity as she could manage. She despised Isla's condescending manner that implied that Julia was just a little country mouse. If she hadn't been a guest at Galbraith Hall, she'd have hurled back a counter-insult about slick city girls who plastered on makeup with a shovel, but it just wasn't worth the trouble, she thought wearily. It would only bring her down to Isla's level of cattiness, and besides, it would make Vince think she really cared about the other girl's taunts. It would boost her importance, and Vince would be sure to think Julia was beginning to feel jealous— and she was never going to give him that satisfaction!

As she went upstairs she heard Andrew telling his sister off for her lack of manners. It was sweet of him, but anyone taken in by Isla's brand of deadly charm deserved all they got. The fact that Vince seemed totally captivated by the other woman was depressing her more by the minute, but she wouldn't let herself think of it. They deserved each other, she thought determinedly.

She changed her clothes, choosing a pale blue sporty blouse and pleated skirt, and she brushed out her hair to a gleaming fall that caressed her shoulders. Then she splashed her cheeks with cool water that tempered them down to a healthy glow. They had no need of makeup to enhance them, but she touched her mouth with lip gloss and held her head high as she went back to join the others.

After lunch it was time to get in the cars for the trip down to Loch Lomond. Vince's car was a two-seater, so naturally Isla went with him, while Andrew drove everybody else in his sister's roomier car. It felt overfull to Julia, though, with Fern breathing down her neck and even James getting animated at the idea of trying out his water skis that afternoon.

"Isla's brilliant," Fern informed Julia. "A good job she likes the water so much since Vince is so keen on it, isn't it? Why don't you have a go?"

"No, thanks." Julia kept the smile fixed on her face. "I've got no wish to make myself look a complete idiot."

"You just carry on looking decorative, Julia," Andrew said gallantly. "I'm not so keen on it, either, so we can hold hands together and let them get on with it."

Vince and Isla were already at the jetty when the others arrived, and the children raced ahead, leaving Julia to feel rather like the older generation as she and Andrew picked their way carefully over the rocking jetty to clamber on to the boat. Isla was down below, changing into her wet-suit, and when she emerged ten minutes later, she looked like something out of a film. No boring black wet-suit for Isla. This one was scarlet, outlining her perfect figure as if it was fused on to her skin. There could hardly be a man alive who wouldn't give her a second or a third glance, and Vince wasn't the kind of man to be slow with his approval. Julia heard him give an admiring whistle as Isla emerged from below deck, and saw her preen herself at his reaction.

"Isn't she gorgeous?" Fern nudged Julia's arm as they lounged against the deck rail waiting for Vince to start up the engine. By now Isla was busily clambering over the side to get herself ready with the water skis, and James hung on to her every word as she gave him brief instructions and advice.

Julia ignored them both and listened instead to Andrew as he pointed out the distant hills to her and told her the general direction of places that had only been names to her until now: the Trossachs, Culloden and its mournful past, the Cairngorm mountains and the royal castle of Balmoral, the Isle of Skye. . . .

"How far is Skye from here, Andrew?" Vince had mentioned the island, she remembered. Something about a descendant of a Galbraith groom with whom he'd corresponded, and that they'd visit there sometime in connection with his research.

"Skye? Oh, I suppose about one hundred and fifty miles or so," Andrew said vaguely. "Maybe less. But well worth the trip if you've a yen to see it. You'll have heard of Dunvegan Castle, of course?"

She looked blank. "Should I have? Is it something important?"

Andrew started to laugh. "It is to a Macleod! It's the seat of the clan chiefs, who've lived there for seven hundred years. It holds many treasures that I'm sure you'd be interested in, Julia, including a lock of Bonnie Prince Charlie's hair and the Fairy Flag."

"Are you having me on?" Julia didn't know

whether he was serious or not, but at this point Vince joined them while they still waited for Isla to get herself organised.

"You'd better not laugh at a Macleod." Vince's voice held a mock severity. "They take themselves very seriously, Julia. And you may think the Fairy Flag is a lot of nonsense, but it's supposed to have magical properties. When it's flown on a battlefield, it makes certain of a Macleod victory, and when it's spread on the marriage-bed, the Macleod chief will be ensured of fertility." He grinned to see the effect his words were having on her now.

"And you believe all this, of course?" She kept a straight face, even though it sounded like a child's fairy story to her.

"Naturally," Andrew said. "It was a gift made to the clan by a fairy, but only to be used in emergencies. The flag has been used in battle twice, and each time the Macleods won. There's no fooling to be done with magic, Julia."

She felt a little shiver run down her spine at the conviction in his voice. She eyed Isla now, ready and waiting to take off on her water skis, poised and controlled in the scarlet wet-suit, completely assured. Whether she was touched with magic or the determination of her clan, Isla Macleod was one formidable lady who wouldn't submit easily to the man of her choice being taken from her. . . . Julia blinked at the way her thoughts were going. As if *she* was the one who was going to step in and lure Vince Galbraith away from this sea goddess! She would have no chance, even if she wanted to—and she most certainly did not!

For the next hour Julia had no time to worry about magic or anything else. She was drenched with spray as the boat suddenly roared off at high speed, and Isla soared behind them, her scarlet figure taut and lithe. The girl could certainly water-ski, Julia thought, with ungrudging admiration. It was a joy to watch her, and then to see how she helped James accomplish his run as well.

"What about the rest of you?" she called through the fine spray the boat swished up as it slowed down. "Are you chicken, Andrew?"

"That's right," he said cheerfully. He put an arm round Julia's damp shoulders. "Anyway, I'm having more fun up here!"

Isla tried to goad Julia into trying out the water skis, but no way was she going to make a fool of herself in front of Vince. . . . It was his reaction, more than any of the others she'd care about. Because of her future position as his assistant, she added hastily to herself.

By late afternoon the water skiers had had enough and Fern was asking impatiently if they couldn't go and have some tea somewhere.

"If you want." Vince gave a sigh. "You'll get as fat as a little pig if you don't stop eating, Fern. Anyway, it'll only be a snack. You and James have to get back to school in a couple of hours, so no messing about so that Thoms has to drive like mad to get you back for supper!"

Andrew spoke eagerly. "How about the rest of us going out for a meal tonight? We may as well finish the weekend in style."

"Oh, I don't know—" Julia began. A cosy foursome with Isla as the other girl wasn't exactly appealing.

"Why not?" Vince was immediately aggressive. "You don't go back to Strathrowan until tomorrow, so you've got no excuse, have you?"

"Perhaps Julia's not used to high living, Vince." Isla nudged him. "It may all be a bit overwhelming for her."

"Not at all. We do have restaurants in Cornwall, Isla." She mentally counted to ten. "We gave up cave-dwelling centuries ago."

She realised that Vince was grinning now as her eyes sparkled with anger. And now who was being the catty one? Julia asked herself!

"That's settled then," Vince said calmly.

"Good." Andrew smiled. "And knowing my precious sister, she'll be needing to doll herself up properly, so when we've fed these little horrors Isla and I had better get back home and meet you two later. We can drop the children back at Galbraith Hall on the way, Vince."

Oh, but that meant she and Vince . . . Julia caught the challenging look on his face, and also the snap of Isla's grey eyes as her brother made the arrangements with which she couldn't very well argue. Soon after four-thirty she found herself beside Vince in the blue two-seater while the others all piled into Isla's car and disappeared in the direction of Glasgow.

"So I have you to myself at last," Vince said. He made no attempt to start the engine immediately.

She was very aware of the subtle scent of his aftershave, and the strong, square-fingered hands as they held the steering wheel. But there was nothing else subtle about the man. His words, whether spoken or silent, always conveyed the same message. Vince Galbraith liked women and he was used to having them fall over just because he looked at them with that dark, brooding, intense look of his. Julia felt her pulse racing as the mouth she couldn't seem to avoid looking at softened into a smile. Oh, yes, she could understand how the mixture of arrogance and tenderness could make a woman go weak, she thought . . . but not this woman. She looked back at him, cool on the surface, though inside her it felt as if a fire was raging. A fire of contempt, she insisted, because this man thought he owned the world with his money and his looks. . . .

"Is that the way you always speak to your employees?" She forced an amused note into her voice. "I can't imagine any of them lasting long."

His face hardened at once. He didn't like being laughed at, and it was a small weapon Julia had discovered instinctively, and intended to use again whenever necessary.

"There are employees and employees," he snapped. "However, if that's how you insist on being treated, so be it. But just remember, you're not in my employ yet. For the present, you're a very desirable young woman, captive in my car, and if you want to get back to Galbraith Hall tonight, you must pay the forfeit."

His annoyance had disappeared again, and she saw the glimmer of a mocking smile on his face as he slid an arm round her shoulders. Her blouse was still damp from the spray of the water, and all through tea she'd been feeling slightly uncomfortable and wishing she could get back to change out of it. Now, as Vince's fingers pressed it even more firmly to her skin, and his eyes appreciated the way the material clung to her figure, she gave a small shudder.

"You know you're a very tantalising young lady, don't you?" His voice was huskily seductive.

"Really? I thought I was a country girl, with the natural look. It only needs the milking-smock—"

"You also jump as if I touch a raw nerve the minute I come near you." His voice was tinged with irritation as he interrupted her. "You don't strike me as being antisocial with Andrew Macleod or my mother, and certainly Meggie always spoke of you in glowing terms. I'd just like to know what you've got against me in particular, Julia."

His nearness was dissolving her resistance with the speed of light, had he but realised it. She couldn't bear him to know it, and to be added to his list of conquests. She resorted to mockery.

"Does it hurt your pride to know that not every female falls under the spell of the Laird of Galbraith? I'd have thought your glamorous blonde was enough for anyone to handle."

He brushed aside the first remarks, but his fingers had tightened on her shoulder at the mention of Isla.

"You needn't take any notice of Isla. She oozes self-confidence, but she's—"

"If you're about to tell me she's got a heart of gold beneath it all, forget it!" Julia interrupted in a brittle tone. "I don't care for her type, and I'm sorry if that offends you."

"Why should it? I'm not Isla's keeper!" he said arrogantly.

Julia glared at him. He was practically her fiancé, by all accounts, but it seemed that was a small matter to him. It didn't stop him chatting up the next available girl! She removed his hand deliberately from her shoulder and sat as far as possible from him in the two-seater, staring directly ahead with her arms primly folded. After a few seconds Vince gave an expressive oath and rammed the car in gear as he started up the engine.

The next minute they were tearing round narrow lanes and steep bends as the car negotiated the twists and turns on the way back to Galbraith Hall. Julia almost shrank back in her seat with fright. Vince was so well acquainted with these roads it was probably perfectly safe, but to her he seemed to be driving like a madman. He was grim-faced and silent. His moods left her limp, and she was beginning to wonder if she'd done the right thing after all in agreeing to work with him. Clearly, there was always going to be a clash of wills between them.

She was relieved when they reached the Hall and the soothing company of Aunt Meg and Rose Galbraith. For two pins Julia would have backed out of the little foursome that evening, but before she could start inventing a headache, Vince had informed his mother that the two of them had plans for the evening.

"So I gather from Fern," Rose said agreeably. "So much the better. Once the children are despatched, Meg and I can have a cosy evening to ourselves."

That seemed to be that, then. Obviously, neither she nor Vince would be missed or wanted that evening. She escaped to her room as quickly as she could.

Julia leaned against her door for a moment, eyes closed, hands clenched. He was impossible, she stormed. An egotistical, hot-tempered clod . . . no, not that . . . you could hardly describe someone so physically superb as a clod. . . . Her cheeks flushed a little as the image of Vince in his Highland rig swept into her mind. He had been truly beautiful, a small voice whispered inside her. Magnificently, aggressively male. . . .

Julia walked purposefully across the room and into the bathroom, peeling off her damp blouse and the rest of her clothes as she ran the water, deliberately pushing all such thoughts out of her mind. She had a quick bath and then flipped through the clothes she'd brought to see what on earth she was going to wear. She couldn't wear the little black dress she'd worn last night. For one thing, she was sure Isla wouldn't be wearing the same dress *she'd* worn before, and for another, Julia couldn't be sure what kind of place Vince would take them to that evening.

Anyway, she didn't have much choice, she thought ruefully, and it would have to be the pale grey crushed velvet skirt and the deep violet evening blouse that went with it. It was an unusual colour combination, but one that suited her perfectly and complemented her colouring, particularly her stunning violet eyes. Or so Aunt Meg had told her when she'd held it up to show her in the cottage at Strathrowan.

After she was dressed and had applied subtle makeup to enhance her eyes even more, Julia stood back and studied the result. She knew she was considering the effect her appearance would have on Vince Galbraith more than anyone else.

She turned abruptly, carrying her grey linen jacket over one arm as she went downstairs. On her feet were high-heeled grey sandals that made her slim legs look longer, and a grey clutch bag finished the total look. She'd have been an idiot if she didn't know she looked good, and Vince's eyes as he waited for her at the foot of the stairs more than told her so. He reached for her hand for a second and she let it rest in his larger one, every nerve in her body touched with a kind of electricity at that moment.

"You're the most beautiful thing that ever came into my life," he said simply, and then he dropped her hand and stood back while she called out her good-byes to the older ladies in the drawing room. His moments of sheer good manners and old-world charm could unnerve her as much as his aggression, she thought unsteadily, but presumably that was the course he had set himself for the evening, and it turned out to be less traumatic than Julia had expected.

Vince drove competently in one of the larger family cars that evening, collecting the Macleods from the flat they shared above the large shop, with Andrew's workshop at the rear. The two men wore dark suits and Isla was dazzling in a simple yellow dress with a brown Shetland stole. Whatever she wore, she'd look fabulous, Julia admitted, but the memory of Vince's words held her in a warm glow all evening so that not even Isla's occasional barbs could touch her.

She'd asked Vince where they were going as they set out on the ride into Glasgow to collect the others. For a second, as she glanced at him, she had seen the gleam of his teeth in the dusky twilight, and he'd taken one hand from the wheel to put it over hers for an instant.

"You and I could reach the stars without even trying, Julia," he'd said very softly, his voice deepening in the way she found so disturbing. "But for tonight we're going to an exclusive little restaurant called Blakie's, where they do marvellous things to fresh salmon. And afterwards, if you're very good, you can try a Gaelic coffee and then we can dance."

She reminded herself that she'd probably be dancing with Andrew, and that that was what she wanted anyway—at least in preference to dancing with Vince. But even as she thought it, she knew it was Vince's arms she wanted to feel round her, to be seduced by the warmth and the music and the little intimate caresses of his hands and his lips. . . . She was slightly shocked at the way her thoughts were going, but when the time came that she slid into his arms and the lights were soft and dim and his lips were brushing her cheek, she gave a small sweet sigh.

"I want you, Julia," he whispered against her skin.

She went rigid in his arms. He was outrageous, she thought weakly. He was supposed to be in love with Isla. . . .

"Don't say such things to me," she said in a low voice. It wasn't fair. . . .

"Why not? Don't you want to hear them? Does it offend you so much? I can't believe you're as innocent as you pretend, nor as cold."

It was hard to pretend anything when they were pressed so close together on the dance floor. She was aware of every sinew of his muscular body, and unable to deny the shooting thrill the knowledge gave her.

"I once told you I wasn't a man-hater," she said in a shaky voice now. "But that doesn't mean I'm ready to throw myself at every man who makes a pass at me, either. It's not very flattering if that's the way you think of me!"

"I've told you how I think of you! Why do you keep pretending this isn't happening to us?" The irritation was back in him again.

Julia bit her lip. If she relaxed her guard for an instant she would be floating high on a cloud in his arms, melting pleasurably against his demanding body. Yielding to him almost without realising it. . . . She'd resisted love for so long, insisting that no other man would break through the glass wall she'd built around her heart since Martin, and no man ever had, until now. . . .

"*Nothing's* happening," she said deliberately.

Vince tightened his hold even more. She was imprisoned in his arms, and every part of him told her he wanted her. . . .

"Isn't it?" he taunted. "What do I have to do to make you respond? Stick pins in you?"

"Just leave me alone," she found herself snapping as the atmosphere of the crowded dance floor and Vince's high-pressure technique became almost unbearable. "I've already said I'll work with you, but that doesn't mean we have to live in each other's pockets, does it?"

"That wasn't what I had in mind, though the idea's quite appealing." His grin faded as she refused to react further.

The music ended and he let go of her abruptly. He still had hold of one hand as he thrust his way through the other couples on the dimly-lit dance floor, most of whom were still oblivious to anything but each other. She knew he was angry with her again, and wished miserably that they didn't always seem to have this effect on each other as they rejoined Isla and Andrew.

"They teach you to dance well in the sticks, Julia. You and Vince made a very lovely couple out there," Isla crooned, but her eyes flashed icily.

"Oh, I've learned quite a lot of things in my time," Julia told her. "Including—"

"Including how to make Isla jealous!" Andrew interrupted with a laugh. "That takes some doing, Julia!"

It hadn't been her intention to do any such thing.

"It's a bit difficult to dance in that crush without getting close to your partner." She was annoyed that she was forced into an explanation that only seemed to make things worse.

"Don't apologise. At least not if I'm going to get the same treatment." Andrew grinned. "My turn next, I hope?"

"Of course." Julia turned to him in relief. He was friendly and uncomplicated, and she needed those qualities around her right now. Andrew was the complete opposite of his caustic sister.

"Julia has different rules for different partners, Andrew," Vince put in abruptly. "You must handle with care!"

The other two seemed unaware of just how much tension there was between her and Vince, Julia thought with relief. She gave her attention wholeheartedly to Andrew for the rest of the evening, knowing the situation would suit Isla perfectly, and she tried not to care as she saw Isla's sinuous shape pressed as close to Vince as a second skin on the dance floor.

She *wouldn't* care, she thought resolutely. But later that night she lay sleepless for hours in the darkness of her room at Galbraith Hall. And she could feel the touch of Vince's lips on her cheek as they moved slowly in time to the seductive music. They hadn't danced together again all evening, but they hadn't needed to. For a little while she had been touched by magic, and the spell hadn't quite dispersed. She tried desperately to rake up the contempt she should feel for a man of his type . . . flirting outrageously with her while Isla, to whom he was practically engaged, glared on. She knew he'd probably discard her as soon as he'd had his fill of her, if ever she was foolish enough to fall for him . . . and she wouldn't. . . .

But she kept remembering his voice . . . together they could reach the stars, he'd told her. Well, she was already there, whether she wanted to be or not. In the darkness of her room she clasped her hands together, feeling the empty place where her engagement ring used to be. She hadn't thought of Martin all evening. It was almost unbelievable to know it . . . and the sudden sighing of the wind outside was like an echo of her own feelings at that moment, and she found that her eyes were damp.

Chapter Five

The misty, ethereal mood had worn off by the next morning. Julia awoke with a throbbing headache and the suspicion that she'd made a fool of herself. She dressed carefully so as not to disturb her head too much and went downstairs stiffly, determined that her rigid control wouldn't slip again.

But she needn't have bothered, because Vince had already left the Hall with his apologies to her and Aunt Meg if they should have left before he returned that afternoon.

"Which we shall have," Aunt Meg said. "I planned on our getting back to Strathrowan before lunch, and we don't want to outstay our welcome."

"You know you could never do that," Rose protested rather regally, but Julia was glad she didn't press them to stay longer, and it was a relief when the two of them were waving good-bye and reversing the journey back toward the picturesque village. It was incredible to think how emotional a weekend it had been, Julia thought suddenly. She hadn't known Vincent Galbraith existed until a few days ago, yet she found him infinitely disturbing to her, whether he angered or outraged her, or was suddenly tender, or aggravated her as he had that morning, when she'd steeled herself up to see him and he'd already left. And without his presence, Galbraith Hall was oddly empty. . . .

"I'm very pleased you accepted Vince's offer to work with him, Julia," Aunt Meg was saying as the old Ford chugged up the steeper inclines of the journey. Julia forced herself to listen and to stop her thoughts rushing wildly on the way they kept doing whenever she thought of Vince's forceful personality. Whether you loved him or hated him, you couldn't be unaware of him, Julia thought weakly, and right now she wasn't prepared to analyse in which category she put herself.

"You think I'm doing the right thing, then?" she murmured.

"I know you are, love," Aunt Meg said stoically. "And don't think I don't understand what the past few months must have been like for you. But you can't go on grieving forever, and Martin wouldn't have wanted you to. A new life among new people is the best way to see everything in the right perspective, and I don't see how you can fail to find the job absorbing."

Oh, yes, the job . . . in Julia's mind it had become almost secondary to the man, and she knew it mustn't be like that. The briefing Vince had given her in his study had revealed that he was serious about his work, and if this sort of chance had been given her with any other employer, she knew she would still have jumped at it. She relaxed a little, feeling some of the tension leave her. She was becoming utterly ridiculous about Vince Galbraith and it was time it stopped. She was acting more like a love-struck schoolgirl than anything else. . . .

"I've arranged to move into the Hall next Monday," she said hurriedly. "I thought we'd have the rest of this week together and next weekend, too."

"Good." Aunt Meg was brisk. "Then we'll work out a programme of things we want to do before you become a working girl again. Though I'll still see something of you, I'm sure, and the games aren't far off, so we'll all be on the move again for those."

"I'm intrigued by the sound of them. What happens exactly?" Julia was glad to talk about something else.

"Oh, the usual highland activities, you know. Tossing the caber and scaling fences and shotputting for some of the heavyweights. Then there are teams of dancers who perform on a special dais and compete for a prize—that's what Fern will be taking part in—a team from her school is competing this year. And the pipe competitions." Aunt Meg started to laugh. "Much as I love the sound of the bagpipes, you never heard such caterwauling as when the individual pipers are all practising their different tunes at the same time before the event begins. Oh, it'll be a day to remember as usual, I've no doubt."

"It sounds it. I'm looking forward to it," Julia told her. And it would be nice to have Aunt Meg there with her instead of just being one of the Galbraith party. For all that Isla kept making her feel like a sassenach from south of the border whenever she could get in a sly dig, Julia's roots were buried staunchly in the highlands as much as anybody else's around here, and the thought of joining in something so traditional kindled an excitement inside her. And a strange kind of pride in the fact that Rose was to present the prizes . . . as if it had anything to do with *her*, Julia thought, but she couldn't quite rid herself of the little glow that Vince's family was held in such high esteem all the same.

For the next week Aunt Meg seemed determined that the two of them should cram in every bit of tourist activity they could, as if Julia was about to emigrate at any minute.

"Oh, I know full well you'll soon be as familiar with the countryside around here as I am myself." Aunt Meg smiled. "But I want to be the one to show you things for the first time, love, so indulge me in that, won't you?"

So together they began an exploration of the old city. Julia was impressed by the mixture of Victorian and Renaissance architecture. The beautiful medieval cathedral dating back to the twelfth and thirteenth centuries was particularly appealing, being the only one of its kind on the Scottish mainland. It gave her a shivery feeling to learn that its site had been a holy place since the original sixth-century church had been built by St. Mungo.

Aunt Meg was a tireless tourist, Julia realised. They browsed in the huge modern shops in Sauchiehall and Buchanan streets, and gazed in amazement at the railway viaduct spanning Argyle Street, which Aunt Meg told her was known as the "Highlandman's Umbrella," because it gave shelter to the poor of the city in times past, and evoked an instant aura of Glasgow's history.

As a breathing space from modern splendours and ancient architecture, they took a picnic lunch to Victoria Park, with its fossilised tree stumps said to be 230 million years old. At Linn Park, on the banks of White Cart Water, they followed the nature trail along paths shaded by tall leafy trees through which the sunlight glinted like gold. In Rouken Glen, they strolled through the cool woods and spacious parkland, and took a small boat out on the lake, where Julia trailed her hand through the clear water.

She was enthralled by the university museum, where there were precious manuscripts and early books, and the paintings of Rembrandt and Whistler. And impressed by their visit to a fifteenth-century mansion with its marvellous treasures, and equally charmed with the Kilbarchan Weaver's Cottage, a typical eighteenth-century weaver's home, with its frugal way of life so evident.

There was so much to do and see, and she fell in

love with everything she saw. Scotland was a land of contrasts, she told Aunt Meg as they returned home exhausted every evening: the mainland and the romantic islands, the mists and mountains, the silver glens and still blue lochs. . . . And she loved it all. . . .

"I couldn't keep this up for much longer," Julia told her aunt on Friday evening. "We must have walked miles of corridors alone this week. Where do you get your energy at your age?"

"It comes from walking the hills." Her aunt laughed. "But hectic or not, it's done you good. You look a different girl from the wishy-washy one who stepped off the train a fortnight ago."

"I feel it," she said. And it was true. There was a relaxing inside her that was like an unravelling of all the tight tensions that had surrounded her since Martin's accident. She could even think of that terrible day now without quite such a searing pain inside her. It was past, and nothing could bring him back. Not that she would ever forget, but the memories were beginning to be less painful, shadowy where they had been so intense, soft and nostalgic where they had been needle-sharp. She hadn't ever fallen out of love with Martin, but she was discovering that love needed to be tended and nurtured like a delicate plant, and if there was no one there on whom to lavish all that love, it very gradually withered and died, quite painlessly in the end. . . .

Maybe if one was very old and lost a partner the feelings would never die, but when the heart was young and life was still beginning, it was normal and natural for it to recover. Even when it had seemed impossible. . . .

The phone rang, dragging Julia out of her philosophical meanderings. She'd been lying back in a comfortable armchair, her eyes closed for a few minutes after making them both a welcome pot of tea, but she jumped up to answer the phone automatically. Of course it wouldn't be for her . . . but it was.

"Andrew? How nice to hear your voice." Her mouth curved into a smile at the sound of his pleasant accent. "Tomorrow night? Yes, I'd love to," she said, responding to her aunt's vigorous nodding. She grinned. Aunt Meg had no idea of what Andrew was saying on the phone, but she'd probably be glad of an evening on her own to recover from the sightseeing week. "All right, I'll be ready about seven o'clock. See you then."

Aunt Meg looked at her expectantly as she hung up.

"He's asked me to a Ceilidh tomorrow night. I said yes, but I haven't got much idea of what to expect!"

Her aunt laughed. "You're in for a treat, then. There'll be plenty of traditional dancing, and some folk singing for everybody to join in, and maybe some poetry reading. It's real 'grass-roots' stuff, Julia. Where is it—did Andrew tell you?"

"Somewhere called the Shieling."

"Oh, well then, you'll want to wear something very informal. Slacks and a shirt. Shieling's the Scots word for summer hut, and I happen to know it's an old converted barn away to the south a bit, but it's very popular with the younger folk. I'm sure you'll enjoy it."

When the time came, she certainly did. She was glad that Aunt Meg had warned her not to dress too formally, because Andrew arrived for her in his own car wearing jeans and a Canadian-style lumber shirt of bright checks. He smilingly approved her cream slacks and multicoloured shirt of pinks and mauves. She'd caught the back of her hair up into a high knot so that it swung above the remaining glossy length of it, which fanned out on her shoulders, and seemed to be just right for a folksy evening. She looked forward to it enormously, and especially in Andrew's company.

He was the least complicated of men, Julia decided. He admired her and told her so with none of the brooding sensuality in his remarks that Vince Galbraith assaulted her with every time they met. The evening was a great success. They joined in the singing with great gusto; Julia caught her breath at the intricate dance patterns the dancers made in traditional highland costume, their soft shoes shuffling miraculously near to the sharp-pointed swords crisscrossed on the floor around which they danced as light as feathers.

Later, the room became hushed and the lights were dimmed. A throaty-voiced Highlander, in kilt and Highland rig, took the centre of the floor, gazing round at the rapt faces for long minutes, the atmosphere so tense it was almost brittle. He was tall and dark-eyed, with fierce red hair and a luxuriant beard, and an air of being at one with the earth. He recited the haunting words of the poems of Robert Burns, and there were many unashamedly damp eyes long before he'd finished. And Julia felt herself stirred by something very basic inside her, knowing this was the land of her ancestors, and that she was a part of them. Feeling again in some strange mystic way that she had come home. . . .

Andrew took her back to the cottage when it was all over and refused to come in for a last drink. He kissed the tip of her nose and told her she'd made the evening come alive for him. Seeing it all through her eyes had given it an added sparkle. Julia floated indoors in a haze of happiness, wondering why such a pleasant man hadn't found himself a wife yet.

Her aunt had heard the car approaching and was in the kitchen making hot chocolate.

"Just for you and me," Julia called out. "Andrew

didn't want to stop, but he said to tell you good-night."

"How did you enjoy it?" Aunt Meg asked eagerly when she brought in the two steaming mugs.

"It was wonderful." Julia said the words with a little sigh. "It made me wish I could stay here forever and be part of it all."

"Why can't you? What have you got to go back for?"

Julia averted her eyes from her aunt's candid ones. There was nothing to go back for. But this cottage wasn't big enough for two, and she couldn't stay at Galbraith Hall for longer than the job took. She wouldn't want to, anyway. But she'd think about it . . . about taking a flat, perhaps, and looking for a job in Glasgow. There was bound to be something in her line. . . .

"You had another phone call while you were out."

"A phone call for *me?*" Her thoughts flew at once to Cornwall, but there was nobody there who'd want to phone her.

"It was Vince." Julia's heart gave a jump at her aunt's words. "He wanted to take you out tonight, as well, and he didn't sound too pleased when I told him Andrew had got in first." She gave a little chuckle. "Vince isn't used to having his nose put out of joint by somebody else. It'll do him good, though I didn't tell him so!"

Yes, it would, Julia thought indignantly. If he'd wanted to take her out he should have arranged it earlier, not rung up late on Saturday night expecting her to be sitting twiddling her thumbs in case he condescended to call! She could imagine the way his handsome face would have darkened when he heard Aunt Meg tell him she'd already gone off with Andrew Macleod. Serve him right. No doubt most girls would have leaped at the chance to be seen out with the eligible Vince Galbraith. . . . She wouldn't let herself admit for a second that there was a stab of disappointment that she hadn't been there when he phoned. That she, too, was woman enough to have enjoyed the envious looks from other girls because she was the one Vince had chosen to escort that evening. . . .

What was she thinking of? she asked herself. Even if she'd been there, she could easily have pleaded a headache or a prior engagement, but she knew darned well she'd have done none of those things. She'd have jumped, the way everyone else jumped. . . .

"Anyway, he said he'll be having you to himself from Monday onwards, so he hoped you'd enjoy Andrew's rustic pleasures."

"I hope he didn't sound as sneering as that!" It had been a refreshing evening, and Julia was angry that Vince Galbraith should have the power to spoil it even without being here.

"Of course he didn't! You seem a mite touchy, love! Vince is as enthusiastic as the next man when it comes to tradition and all the ancient folklore. If he wasn't, he'd probably have persuaded Rose to modernise Galbraith Hall by now or turned it into a tourist attraction with a pay-desk and guides and gift shop, and a safari park in the grounds!" Aunt Meg shuddered at the thought, and Julia admitted that Vince would never do that. She knew it without having to be told.

"Anyway," her aunt was chuckling again and looking at Julia with a knowing look in her eyes, "he was just jealous, that's all, and sometimes his tongue runs away with him when he's wound up."

"Jealous! Because I'd gone out with Andrew, you mean?" Julia started to laugh. "Don't be daft. He could have his pick of a hundred girls, I bet." And proably had, she thought ruefully.

"Maybe. But tonight he wanted you!"

She had no answer to that. She finished her

chocolate and said she was going to turn in. She was suddenly very tired. It had been an exciting evening, but the past week had caught up with her, too, and it was as much as she could do to cream her face and crawl into the cool sheets, leaving the curtains pulled back as she liked to do, to see the sky and the stars and the hazy distant mountains. . . .

And off in their direction was Galbraith Hall. It was the house she was interested in, she told herself firmly. That beautiful house with all its treasures, both monetary and aesthetic, and not the man. But it was the man's face that kept intruding into her thoughts all the same. The image of a tall, dark man with the breeze ruffling his hair and dark, brooding eyes with dancing hazel flecks in them when he wanted to be at his most charming . . . eyes that could snap like a tiger's when he didn't get his own way.

And his mouth . . . Julia stirred restlessly in the narrow bed, her arm unconsciously flung across her pillow, curling it into herself. Suddenly remembering Vince's mouth so vividly, and the way it had felt when it was pressed to hers . . . Knowing again the sensation of hearing words spoken only a hair's-breadth from her lips . . . Feeling the yearning deep inside her to know it again . . . Her cheek pressed into the pillow as if it was Vince's cheek; her arms curled around it more tightly; her body moved restlessly seeking fulfillment . . . wanting his arms to be holding her and crushing her. . . .

She heard her aunt's footsteps on the twisting, creaking staircase and relaxed her hold on the pillow. She was breathing rapidly, and she ran her tongue around lips that were suddenly dry.

"Oh, no," she whispered to herself. "I won't let him affect me this way. I won't think of him. I won't want him. . . ."

But she *did*, and no amount of arguing with

herself was going to deny the fact. The only thing she could do was to despise him for the way he'd thrown his animal magnetism at her when, according to Fern, he was practically engaged to Isla Macleod. When the two of them had spent a weekend together only this summer . . . Julia felt her heightened emotions begin to cool down.

She'd forgotten that, she thought furiously. How many more weekends had the two of them spent together before that one? And how many other girls had he treated to his charms in the same way? Stolen weekends . . . afternoons on his boat . . . entertaining them at the Hall, perhaps, while Rose was abroad and the children away at school . . . he had it made, Julia thought angrily. The perfect setup for seduction, and she'd almost let herself fall for it, too. She'd almost let herself admit that she was falling in love with him. . . .

"Oh, I forgot to tell you last night that Vince will be coming for you on Monday morning, Julia. He wants to pick up some books from an antiquarian bookshop in Glasgow, and he thought you'd like to see the place as well."

"Fine," Julia said coolly. She thought she had her control back in place now. She was going to be working with the man, so one more car ride wasn't going to turn her poise inside out. She tried to put him at the back of her mind as Aunt Meg suggested they go to the service at the village kirk that morning, and afterwards introduced her to several of her acquaintances as they stood around chatting in the sunlit kirkyard.

It didn't upset her anymore, Julia realised suddenly. She'd once had a passion for looking at old tombstones, but after Martin died she related such places only to him. Now, she realised, she was studying the ancient Gaelic writing on the weathered headstones of the tiny kirkyard with as much interest as she had ever done. It was only when she saw a small bush of brilliant yellow gorse growing bravely in one corner against the dry stone wall that she felt a soft pang inside.

I won't forget you, Martin, a small voice said pleadingly inside her, *but there's no kissing time for us anymore. And I need to live. . . .*

When the Galbraith car arrived for her on Monday morning, Julia saw that it was Thoms, the chauffeur, who eased his burly figure out of the driver's seat and walked up the drive to knock on the cottage door. After she'd steeled herself to see Vince, she raged, hardly realising that her anger was mixed with disappointment. She must be half-enjoying their verbal battles, she told herself, but all the same, the fact remained that now she'd have to make small talk with this man instead of seeing the antiquarian bookshop that her aunt had mentioned.

"Mr. Galbraith apologises for not coming himself, Miss." Thoms touched his green chauffeur's cap in greeting. "The books he ordered haven't arrived yet, so he didn't need to go into Glasgow after all."

So he didn't think it was worth the journey just to fetch her! Julia lifted her chin a little higher and said it didn't matter at all, and the family limousine would be far more comfortable anyway. She showed Thoms where she'd left her suitcases and waited while he put them in the boot of the car. Then she hugged Aunt Meg, feeling suddenly as if she was deserting a sinking ship, since she'd come to Scotland to stay at Strathrowan.

As if she sensed the sudden emotion, Aunt Meg spoke briskly. "Good Lord, girl, anyone would think you were going a thousand miles away instead of barely twenty! At least you'll be practically on my doorstep instead of all that way away in Cornwall, and I'll be seeing you often, I hope! Phone me tonight to let me know you've settled in all right, though I'm sure Rose will phone as well."

She probably would, Julia thought with a smile, remembering her aunt's endless phone calls. She slid into the front seat beside the chauffeur, as it seemed a bit silly to sit in the back on her own and arrive as if she was royalty, and waved to her aunt until the cottage was out of sight and they were on their way to Galbraith Hall.

And after all, it wasn't so difficult to talk to Thoms. The worst thing was following his accent, which was very strong and not always easy to understand. He rolled his r's in such an exaggerated way that his tongue must still be vibrating five minutes later, Julia thought in fascination, but she gradually got used to it and didn't need to listen so intently.

For his part, Thoms was intrigued by her soft Cornish lilt. He'd never been south of the border, nor too far south of Glasgow, since Mrs. Galbraith either flew when she went abroad or occasionally took a ship from Stranraer. His duties were mainly local or northerly, but he liked the look of this little lass.

She was more natural than some of the flightly ones who flashed their lashes at the boss. That Miss Macleod, for instance. Thoms didn't like that one at all, with her quick answers and heavy makeup. A good-looker, all right, and a figure to set a man drooling, but he much preferred the softness of the little lass sitting next to him now. He liked softly rounded girls with gentle faces and big, lustrous eyes. And these particular eyes were such an unusual colour . . . yes, Thoms decided. He definitely approved of this one. . . .

"Have you worked for the Galbraiths long, Thoms?" Julia asked him as they started on the last climb toward the Hall, and her nerves began to get a bit jittery.

"Oh, aye, Miss. About as long as I can mind," he said. "And me faither before me was in the Galbraiths' employ. He worked for old Mr. Galbraith, the present one's father, as a farm manager."

"Farm manager?"

"Oh, aye, the Galbraiths hold much of the land around this area. The boss has quite a busy time of it, keeping track of it all. There are four farms in the valley, and two more hill farms that are all answerable to the estate, though managed independently, of course."

Thoms spoke with quiet pride, and Julia realised that there was more to Vince than she had suspected after all. Though he was still as conceited as ever, she added hastily. And still as much a womaniser, and arrogant . . . and still as dishy. . . .

The limousine purred smoothly to a halt outside Galbraith Hall, and Julia stepped out. It seemed odd to think that she was arriving this time as part of the household instead of just a visitor. She couldn't quite get used to the idea, but her brief moment of uncertainty ended as the door opened and Rose Galbraith appeared to greet her graciously.

"I've told Vince off for not meeting you himself, Julia," she said at once. "But there's been a bit of trouble with sheep straying on one of the hill farms, and every man was needed, including Vince."

Thoms hadn't told her that—if he'd known about it. Julia felt slightly better. It also meant he wasn't here at the moment, and it gave her a little breathing-space to unpack her suitcases when Thoms had taken them to her room, and then to join Rose for coffee. The maze of corridors was no more familiar than it had been before, but in time she hoped to find her way about. She'd already wandered into a large, rather austere room filled with armour, thinking it was the drawing room, and was smiling about it to Rose as her hostess poured out the coffee from an elegant Georgian coffeepot.

"I'm surprised Vince didn't take you in there last time you were here, Julia. There are some quite interesting things in there, including a very old Claymore reputed to have been given to the family by James the first—the Poet King, as they called him."

"Is that the great sword over the fireplace?" Julia said.

"That's the one."

Julia started at the sound of Vince's voice. Neither of them had heard him arrive, and she turned quickly to see him stride across the drawing room and drop into a chair, regardless of the fact that his jeans were muddy and there was a streak of dirt across his cheek. He looked more vulnerable than she'd ever seen him, Julia thought, as he blew out his cheeks with weariness and told them that the sheep had given them all a merry chase that morning.

"They don't move all that fast, but when there are a couple of hundred of them all spreading about in different directions and scenting freedom, even the dogs are hard put to cope with them," he commented. "Coffee is just what I need, Rose."

He drained his cup in one go and held it out for a refill, looking at Julia in a relaxed, friendly way for once, with no obvious undertones in his voice.

"James the first was the king who said his daughter had a face like starlight, in case you didn't know it." He suddenly raised his coffee cup to Julia. "A pity he's not around to see yours, my bonnie lass!" Before she could think whether to be embarrassed or suspicious of his remark, he'd got to his feet and told them he was off to shower and change, then he'd be with them for lunch.

"And then you and I can get down to business," he said directly to Julia. "We'll spend this afternoon in the study going over the stuff I've already collated and you can tell me where I'm going wrong."

There was a slight mocking note in his voice as he'd finished talking and left the room. Just as if anybody would dare to tell him any such thing, Julia thought instantly. She doubted if anybody ever had—until now. But there had to be a first time for everything.

Chapter Six

Later, when they were seated in the study, he pulled out sheafs of paper and notes, and spread them over the huge desk. He sat beside Julia to go through the notes systematically, giving total concentration to his work. Julia liked that in a man, and knew she could quickly become as absorbed in Vince's project as he was.

"How long have you been working on it?" she asked him.

He gave a small groan. "It seems like forever, but it's been about two years, on and off. I just haven't got round to putting it all in order. There are still gaps in my research, especially around the 1830s, but I hope to put a lot of that right when I see this old crofter on Skye."

"He really does exist, then?" She didn't really know why she said it, but Vince's eyebrows drew together in a frown.

"Naturally he exists! There's no need for you to mistrust everything I say, Julia. Anyway, you'll find out for yourself when we leave for Skye on Friday."

"*This* Friday?"

He leaned back in his chair. "Have you some other engagement that's more important?" His voice was heavy with sarcasm, and she flushed. He was the boss, and when he said jump, she was supposed to jump. . . .

"No, of course not," she said crossly. "You just took me by surprise, that's all."

"I seem to have a habit of doing that. You might as well realise that this is no conventional job, Julia. I may be missing for much of the time when I'm needed on estate business, but I'll expect you to be ready at a minute's notice when I need you."

Wasn't that just the way she'd expect him to be . . . ?

"Thanks for warning me." She hoped she didn't sound as sarcastic as he did.

"If it bothers you, now's the time to pull out—"

"I've no intention of doing so!" Julia said at once.

Vince looked at her for a long minute. "Good. At least that sounded almost convincing. You realise it will mean an overnight stay on Skye, of course, but there are perfectly respectable hotels in Portree. So now we understand each other—and no previous engagements to invent—right?"

Julia felt her face redden again, wondering if her expression had given her away at that moment when he'd mentioned the overnight stay on Skye. For a second the idea had flashed into her mind that it would be almost comparable with Isla's "weekend away with him" that Fern had spoken of, barely veiling her hints as to its purpose. Almost . . . She chose to ignore his jibe.

"I haven't been here long enough to have any 'previous engagements,' as you put it. I might have gone over to Strathrowan, though, to see Aunt Meg. I didn't know I'd have to be on duty weekends as well."

"I was thinking more of Andrew Macleod. Don't tell me he hasn't asked you out again."

"He hasn't, as a matter of fact." His manner irritated her. What difference did it make to Vince Galbraith if Andrew had asked her out? Or if she was going out with the whole Macleod clan on a binge, come to that?

Vince was shuffling papers together and glancing at his watch. "I'm glad. Outside involvements are always a bad influence on a successful working partnership." His voice was cool and egotistical again. As if anyone who worked with him should have nothing else on their minds at all but the man and the job. Not just during office hours, but totally. At least that was the impression Julia got, and it suddenly incensed her. Why shouldn't she see Andrew or anyone else if she wanted to? She certainly would. Anyway, she *did* have an "outside involvement." She had Martin. . . . She held her chin high and looked Vince in the eye, as cool as he was.

"I didn't say I didn't have an involvement with anyone. I merely said Andrew hadn't asked me out again—yet."

His hand reached out and rested on her shoulder. It felt heavy, the pressure of his fingers digging into her skin, so that she was sure there would be indentations there later. But she resisted the urge to jerk away as he leaned toward her, and the tang of his aftershave, fresh as the salt breeze of a storm-swept sea, tingled in her nostrils. His face was close, the hazel flecks in his dark eyes caught by the sunlight from the window. There was a sudden ruthless look about his mouth that unnerved her slightly.

"I told you once, I'm used to getting what I want, Julia." His voice was softly confident. "I don't need to play games, although the thought of that has delightful connotations. . . ."

"I've no intention of playing games," she said tightly, wishing he wouldn't keep looking at her in that slightly mocking way that sent butterflies racing round inside her. "I've come here to work and if you're not satisfied with that . . ."

"Oh, I'm quite sure you'll be satisfactory—in every way."

She couldn't miss his double meaning and was furious with herself for reacting, feeling her neck go hot and knowing the colour was climbing high in her cheeks. Then he laughed softly again and moved away from her. Julia immediately felt as if she had wilted visibly, but he was walking round the other side of the desk now, with that rangy stride of his that she couldn't help comparing to an animal stalking its prey. And she was the next victim, she thought dizzily, if he had his way. . . .

Thank goodness he hadn't pursued her remark about being involved with someone else, she thought suddenly. She didn't want to start explaining, but if it ever came to it, she hoped she'd be able to talk rationally about Martin by now. She felt that she could, now that time and distance had relieved the sharp ache of bereavement. It had been happening for some time, she thought, but until coming to Strathrowan and finally cutting herself off from the past, she hadn't wanted to accept it. And finally realising that her life hadn't ended because Martin had died was like a clean, invigorating surge of fresh air into her lungs.

"If you want to take your time browsing through the notes I've already made for the rest of the afternoon, please do so." Vince was businesslike again now, and she breathed a little sigh of relief. "I have an engagement this evening, so if I don't see you until breakfast tomorrow morning, we'll leave for Glasgow around ten o'clock. But just before I leave you, come along to the library and see my special treasure. It's very valuable and kept under lock and key. You'll find the notes on it, but I'm sure you'd like to take a good look at it."

He held the door open for her and she felt his hand rest lightly on her elbow as he guided her along the corridor. It wasn't necessary, she wanted to protest. She wasn't made of china . . . but all the same, she had to admit it gave her an oddly cherished feeling, as if she was as fragile as the delicate pieces of porcelain in the Galbraith collection. Let him think of her like that, she grinned to herself. He'd find out that she was as tough as Aunt Meg inside. . . .

She'd noticed the small square table at one side of the library when she'd wandered in here before when she and her aunt had been house guests. It stood against one wall, between the tall bookcases, and Vince took a key from his pocket and unlocked it. The lid of the table lifted up to reveal a glass-topped interior. Julia gasped as she looked inside. There was an exquisite ivory chess set, and she felt the excitement stirring inside her as her expert's eyes began assessing it.

"My goodness," she breathed. "It looks—"

"It's Norse." Vince confirmed what had already been spinning in her mind. "It's quite unique, and was said to belong to a man called Varfa, a Norse sea-pirate, one of the early invaders who was apparently captivated by the beauties of Loch Lomond and the mountains, and settled here, fading into obscurity from then on. He could very well have been one of our ancestors, and I personally find it a more believable tale than the lone piper haunting the place. That's a tale for tourists and gullible house guests, but Varfa was real enough. I like to think there's a little of his spirit in all of us."

Julia was hardly listening, especially when the teasing note came into his voice. when he spoke of gullible house guests. The chess pieces weren't perfect, and she would not expect them to be. There were tiny chips on some and several of the noses on the ivory faces had been flattened or scratched. She could imagine the flamboyant Norsemen hurling them across a room in their fury at reaching checkmate. Her eyes were drawn slowly to Vince's, and he could see the excitement shining there.

She watched him lift the glass cover, not realising how her beautiful violet eyes were goading him to an almost raging desire.

"I wouldn't let everyone touch Varfa's chess set." He spoke harshly in an attempt to dampen the feelings she stirred in him. She took his words as a slur.

"I'm not just anyone, remember? I'm your assistant. If you don't let me see all the pieces you want included in the work I won't be able to do my job properly."

"And that would never do—"

"I thought that was the object of our relationship." Julia had the strangest feeling that for once she had the upper hand, though she couldn't explain why. But it wasn't often it happened where this man was concerned.

He let her handle the old pieces of the chess set. She picked them up reverently, her slim fingers tracing the detailed workmanship, the intricate crowns, the swords, the masklike faces with their blank eyes and squat bodies.

"Norsemen were aggressive, weren't they?" she breathed. "They had an inborn need to be hunters—" She stopped, remembering that Vince seemed firmly convinced that Varfa the sea-pirate was one of his own ancestors. She heard him give a soft laugh.

"Go on!" he invited. "So that's where my character originates, is it? Is that what you were about to say?"

"I wouldn't be so presumptuous. I've never tried to analyze your character," she lied, her tone implying it was something on which she wouldn't waste her time.

"You disappoint me, then. I thought every red-blooded young woman liked to think she was worthy of being hunted—the chosen one!"

"Some of us prefer the more subtle approach," Julia said cuttingly. "He-man tactics can be very boring."

Vince took the chess pieces from her hands and replaced them, closing the lid with as much firmness as he dared. His voice was cold, his mouth a tight line.

"Some of you deserve to end up on the shelf. Isn't that the quaint old expression they used to use? You seem to be a prime candidate, Miss Chase. A man could grow old trying to get past that prickly exterior, and if he had any sense, he'd soon give up trying!"

"So there you are." Rose's voice broke into the chilling silence between them. Julia turned thankfully away from Vince's hard face as his mother entered the library, the usual gracious smile on her lips.

"I thought you'd still be deep in discussion in the study," Rose went on. "But I see Vince couldn't resist showing you Varfa's chess set!"

"Did you want us for anything in particular, Rose?" Vince's voice had a touch of impatience in it.

"Oh, yes! Isla's just been on the phone to say she's finishing early this evening and Andrew will be minding the shop until closing time, so if you want to pick her up any earlier, she can be ready by six o'clock."

"Good," he said briefly. "That means six-thirty, knowing how long it takes her to get ready. We've finished here for the day anyway—at least, I have. Julia's going to go through my notes."

"Well, first she can come and have some after-noon tea," Rose said indignantly. "You're not going to start your dictatorial ways already, Vince, so you just get off upstairs and do whatever you had in mind, and Julia can take a little break with me!"

Julia hardly dared glance at Vince as he strode out

of the library without a backward glance or another word. No one would dare speak to him like that except Rose! But he'd certainly been right about one thing this wasn't exactly a conventional job, Julia realised. And she wouldn't mind betting that if Vince decided to carry on working until midnight, he'd expect her to be right there on the other side of the desk, as absorbed as he was himself. She probably would be, too . . . but just now, he gave a laugh at his mother's words, and told her that was one thing he wasn't hanging around to hear.

What had she expected this evening to be like? A continuous discussion on the proposed book he was working on? All of them sitting in cosy domesticity around the colour television, discussing the price of fish? She didn't quite know what she'd expected, but the one thing she'd least wanted to hear was that Vince would be going out with Isla Macleod on her first evening at Galbraith Hall. It was so illogical as to be downright ludicrous, but the fact remained that she did care, and the next fact to strike her was to wonder just how she *was* going to spend the evening in front of her.

She followed Rose into the drawing room, where a silver tray was spread with tea cups and thin slices of cake and biscuits. Julia felt suddenly awkward. She shouldn't be entertained like this, should she? She was, after all, an employee of the house. As if in answer to her unspoken question, Rose indicated a luxurious chair and poured the tea with no formality.

"I don't want any nonsense between us about you being in Vince's employ, Julia," she said coolly. "As far as I'm concerned, you're the niece of my old friend, and I'm more than pleased to have you staying in the house. It's refreshing to hear another English voice, too."

She handed Julia a wafer-thin plate and the tray of biscuits.

"I'm not too sure what my role is supposed to be," Julia began helplessly, and Rose smiled at once.

"Well, as I don't either, what does it matter? As long as you're on hand when Vince wants to work on his project, I'm sure that'll be good enough for him. It will be pleasant to have another woman in the house.

"You had a job that you enjoyed very much, I take it?" Rose went on smoothly. "But I imagine if you'd been in it for some time you must have seen every stately home around in the West of England. Meg did tell me that's what your Mr. Pollard liked to do."

Julia laughed. "Well, not the homes of the aristocracy, so much, though he was as keen to browse through them as any tourist. But he was very keen on going out and about, as he liked to call it, and finding pieces at the source, instead of waiting for people to come into the shop and bring them to us. It was a far more interesting way of going about things." She suddenly looked down into her cup. "You must wonder why I ever wanted to leave it."

"Not at all. It never does anyone any harm to follow a sudden whim, and one can get in a terrible rut even when doing a job one likes. A change and a new challenge can do nothing but good, in my opinion."

"I'm sure I shall enjoy working on Vince's project with him, anyway. It's always a pleasure to work with someone who has a great enthusiasm for his work."

"He certainly has that, and I'm sure you were the answer to a prayer," Rose nodded. "My son is the kind of man who works hard and plays hard, as you'll discover. There are no half-measures about him."

Julia felt a little shiver run through her. He would be a demanding employer. She'd already guessed that. And demanding in other ways too. . . . She remembered the way he'd told her he wanted her, but there had hardly been any need to put it into words. . . .

The door opened and he was there, looking as immaculate as ever, no matter what he wore. This time it was a conventional dark suit with a pale blue silk shirt and dark tie. Julia felt a twist of envy for any girl who would be seen out with Vince Galbraith and refused to admit that the feeling was nearer to jealousy because that girl was Isla Macleod. . . .

"Have a nice evening," he said softly to the two of them. Just as if he knew exactly what she was feeling, Julia thought instantly. Just as if he stood there, posing for effect like some male model in a department store. Only with more devastating effect. . . .

The next second he was gone, and minutes later they heard the roar of his car engine and the diminishing sound as it moved away in the direction of Glasgow. Julia felt a sudden brief loneliness as the sound died away, and shook herself mentally. What did it matter to her if he was living it up in some dim-lit cellar restaurant with the glamourous Isla? She just wished she could get the two of them out of her mind. She put her cup and saucer back on the silver tray and told Rose she thought she'd do a little more browsing through Vince's notes before dinner.

Did Rose expect her to change? she suddenly wondered. Just how formally was the household run at Galbraith Hall? He should be here to tell her these things, she raged inside. He had no right to leave her like this. . . .

As if she read her thoughts, Rose leaned forward and patted her knee, making her feel like an idiotic schoolgirl as she guessed her feelings must be showing all over her face.

"You must treat the place as your home while you're here, Julia. We don't dress up for dinner, unless you feel you want to freshen up into another dress. Otherwise, we live perfectly informally. And if you want to watch television or read or anything else, there's a little sitting room at the end of the corridor on your floor where you'll find everything at your disposal. It's a guest sitting room, though Vince sometimes uses it, too. Or feel free to join me here, if you wish. I intend listening to a concert on the radio this evening, a charity piano recital from Glasgow. That's where Vince and Isla have gone tonight, and between you and me, it's not really his thing at all, but he was pleased to add his name to the list of patrons."

She gave a little chuckle as she spoke, and Julia felt a surge of relief that, after all, there wasn't going to be an intimate little dinner for two for Vince and Isla that evening. She was becoming more and more irrational every time she thought of him, she thought irritably. He was really beginning to get under her skin.

She left Rose to wander back to the study and try to clarify some of Vince's erratic notes. He knew what he wanted to do, but some of the data was still in a haphazard muddle. She began the job of sorting it, but gave up after an hour or so. The end of the day wasn't the best time, and it would be a lot easier if he were there. She gave up eventually, went upstairs and washed and changed into a light summer dress of turquoise blue. It was one of her prettier ones, and she wore it almost as a gesture of defiance, because Vince wasn't there to see her in it and let those brooding eyes wander over her shape. She wasn't sure what she was trying to prove.

After dinner she opted out from listening to the radio concert and found the small sitting room with the TV and everything a guest could possibly want for private entertainment. And for the first time since coming to Galbraith Hall, she relaxed as she laughed at the antics of a ridiculous American comedian who was nonetheless very clever . . . but she couldn't relax entirely, because the strains of the piano music drifted upward from time to time from the open windows below, and she could still imagine Vince and Isla, their faces rapt in a shared experience. And later, there would surely be a candlelit meal . . . a man like Vince wouldn't do any less. And later still . . . ?

She was very tired, she discovered, and went to bed fairly early. But she couldn't sleep, and though she insisted to herself that she wasn't listening for the sound of a car engine roaring up to the house, her ears were alert when it finally came. And to the careful shutting of the car door, the footsteps along the corridor into the room next to hers, the soft creaks and movements as Vince prepared for bed. Julia turned her head in the pillow, to blot out the sounds, and to try and convince herself that she couldn't care less whether he was at this very moment reliving an evening with Isla, and whatever delights that held for him. She didn't care, she insisted silently . . . but she did.

The following morning they drove into Glasgow to the antiquarian bookshop. While they were intent on working, Julia felt a lot easier in Vince's company. There was none of the antagonism between them that seemed to spark so rapidly, nor the unsubtle seduction treatment she found so unnerving. And the bookshop was an Aladdin's Cave to her. They spent more than an hour just browsing among the musty old books, and then collected the ones the manager had obtained for Vince's research.

"We'll take a look at Isla's shop while we're here," he said when they emerged into the sunlight again. Julia's heart jolted. She didn't particularly want to, but she could hardly refuse. Besides, he probably wanted to see her himself, and the thought sent her spirits plunging a little.

He drove them through a maze of streets until they came to a small green oval set with shrubs and trees, around which were some exclusive little shops, selling clothes and paintings and high-class pottery and glassware. In the centre of them was a long shop-front saying, simply, Macleod.

"I'm impressed," Julia forced herself to say.

"Oh, Isla's a canny lass," Vince told her. "She knows what she wants and the right way to get it. She built the business up in a little more than three years from a very modest little concern."

She knows what she wants all right, Julia thought, as soon as they stepped inside the plushly carpeted shop. Isla was talking to a customer, but she handed her over to an assistant at once, and walked across to Vince on high-heeled shoes, to slip a hand through his arm. She looked beautiful in sunshine yellow, her lips and fingernails a complementary bronze, and Julia immediately felt as if she paled beside her, even though she was particularly fond of her own sea-green suit that Vince had complimented her on that morning.

Watching the two of them now, she felt a wild stab of jealousy as Isla reached up and touched Vince's cheek with her bronze lips, as if she had every right to do so.

"Darling, how marvellous! I haven't stopped telling Andrew about last night's concert yet. Wasn't it wonderful?" Her eyes looked directly into Vince's, her voice breathy on the last word, all intended to convey that it wasn't only the concert she was talking about, Julia thought at once. She was very clever, and it was several minutes before she turned to speak to Julia, as if she had been so enraptured at seeing Vince she had only just remembered her.

"Julia, you must forgive me," she said coolly. "It's not often Vince calls in here, and we always have so much to talk about. Which is quite silly, as we only saw each other last night!"

Thank you. I knew that, Julia thought silently.

"I thought Julia would be interested in seeing the

place," Vince said easily. There was a hint of laughter in his voice now, and Julia realised instantly that he could see through Isla's guile, and that he also sensed the way her feathers were ruffled. The typical chauvinistic male. . . .

"It's a pity Andrew's not around. I'm sure he'd love to see you, Julia." Isla's manner changed subtly. Clearly, an interest in her brother was more acceptable than one in Vince Galbraith, whom she looked on as her property. Maybe Fern hadn't been just catty, Julia thought. Maybe these two *were* as good as unoffically engaged. Isla certainly chose to give that impression, even if Vince's behaviour at times suggested otherwise.

She followed the other two through the shop with its bales of glowing tartans and racks of made-up garments of every description, highlighted here and there by an intricate silver medallion or bracelet draped carefully across to give the best effect. She felt rather like a pet poodle trotting along at their heels, and tried to push the feeling down.

"I'm sorry to miss Andrew, too. We hit it off so well the other night," she said coolly, and saw a sudden tightening of Vince's jaw at her words.

Almost as if he was jealous, she thought in astonishment, but with him, of course, it would be something even more basic than jealousy. He just couldn't bear to think a woman could be interested in another man when he was on the scene.

"He was talking about seeing you next Saturday evening," Isla went on carelessly.

Before Julia could answer, Vince spoke crisply. "Providing we're back from Skye in time. Don't forget, Julia's a working girl now, and we've business to attend to as well as pleasure."

"You're not keeping her working all weekend, too, are you, Vince?" Isla said with a flash of annoyance on her face. Vince said shortly that they were starting out for Skye on Friday, and it was anybody's guess when they'd get back on Saturday.

There was a sudden tension between the three of them, and for a moment Julia felt all the force of the Celtic races concentrated in those four walls in an unspoken battle of wills. And she was somehow caught up in the middle. . . .

Chapter Seven

Julia told Isla she'd ring Andrew the minute they got back from Skye on Saturday so that he could come and pick her up, and ten minutes later she and Vince were driving back through Glasgow and out toward the hills in the direction of Galbraith Hall. They drove in silence for most of the way. Vince was in a sullen mood, and Julia had no intention of forcing him into conversation. He was like a child who couldn't get his own way, she thought, and the novelty of it would do him good.

When they were still some distance from the Hall, he suddenly pulled the car onto the side of the road. What now? she began to wonder, as her heart started banging in her chest. The big seduction scene . . . ?

He opened the car door and came round to open hers. She stepped outside, not quite sure what was happening. The air was pure and still, the hillsides fertile and green along this particular stretch, dotted with sheep that looked as if they were painted on a giant green canvas. There were white-painted farmhouses and the darker masses of trees. Here and there were the glowing yellow patches of gorse. Julia caught her breath. It was a beautiful, heart-stopping scene. If her eyes moved farther afield they caught the first glimpse of Loch Lomond, not fully in view yet, and the towering blue-grey mountains surrounding it. It was an artists' paradise, she thought again.

"Those are the Galbraith farms," Vince said, sweeping his arm around to encompass everything they could see below them.

"I'm stunned," Julia said truthfully. She'd had no idea the Galbraiths owned so much land.

"As impressed as you were by Macleod's jewellery?"

"There's hardly any comparison, is there . . . ?" Her words died away at the look in his eyes. *Exactly,* they said, and she knew she'd given him just the response he wanted. The man was impossible. . . .

"I like Andrew," she spoke deliberately, looking him squarely in the eyes. "Does that bother you?"

Her eyes challenged him. They glowed with annoyance, exasperation, and the sparkle of a fight. They were intensely violet at that moment, fringed with long dark lashes that matched her hair. Her cheeks glowed, too, with the fire that he always managed to stir up inside her, and her soft red lips were slightly parted as she waited for his verbal retaliation. Her long dark hair streamed out behind her in a sudden small gust of wind, and before she could guess his intention he suddenly caught her in his arms.

"Yes, it bothers me." He spoke softly, his face very close to hers. "Like you've bothered me ever since I set eyes on you, Miss Julia Chase. And I've wanted you from the very first minute when you whirled round with the Ravenscroft piece clutched carefully in your hands, those beautiful eyes wide with surprise and indignation."

Her mouth was suddenly dry at the naked desire in his voice and in the eyes that burned into hers. She could feel the strength of his body pressing against hers as he pinned her against the car. She was unable to deny the ecstatic sensations washing over her as his hands caressed her. She was just as unable to stop herself from kissing him back. . . .

"You drive me to distraction with your prim little ways," he said roughly against her mouth.

His undeniable sex appeal oozed from every pore of him. Julia made no attempt to pull away. It was as if an invisible silken cord held her captive in his arms. Such a willing captive . . .

"You do your share of driving me wild, too." She spoke shakily, on an intake of breath, and suddenly their mouths were only a whisper apart.

"Then why do you keep up this pretence that it means nothing to you, Julia? Why should we go on playing these games? Haven't I made it plain enough that I want you?"

Oh, he'd made it all too plain, she thought dizzily. But there was a world of difference between merely wanting someone physically and loving them. Without love the wanting wasn't enough. . . . For a moment longer she let the enchantment of his seduction flood her senses. His hands were roaming sensuously over her body and bringing a response that left her weak. She wanted him, too. She came to life under his caressing hands as they brushed her breasts in those tantalising movements, her nipples hardening involuntarily. He could bewitch her. . . .

The sound of another car approaching slowly up the sharp incline of the road made him loosen his hold on her reluctantly. Julia felt as if she was in a slowly unwinding spiral as her eyes focussed on the sensual face so close to hers. Seconds passed before he let her go, touching her lips with his own, and she could hear the note of triumph in his voice.

"Now try telling me you don't want me, when every little bit of you is saying otherwise!"

Julia's legs were suddenly weak, and she almost stumbled inside the car. The erotic feelings he'd awoken in her were dwindling fast and being replaced by rage—rage at him for exposing her own weakness so blatantly. She pulled the car door shut behind her with an angry gesture. By the time Vince slid in beside her, she had full control of herself again.

"Do you think we could just stick to business in future, Vince? I think it's best if we each stick to our own private lives. I do have a life of my own, you know. You're not the be-all-and-end-all of my existence—" She was beginning to babble as she caught the glitter in his dark eyes.

"I will be," he assured her ruthlessly. The next minute the car shot forward in its usual style, and Julia felt as if her head was being pulled back against the seat by an invisible G-force.

"As soon as work on your book is finished, I shall leave Galbraith Hall," she said in a clipped voice. The words were out before she could stop them, but they had to be said. It was the only way she could cope with things. . . .

"Running away?" he asked grimly. "That must mean something significant, I'd say."

"Just don't bother reading too much into it, or you may not like what you see," she snapped back.

Blast him! A woman would have to be made of wood to be unaffected by him! And Julia was anything but that. An ice-maiden, he'd called her, but the ice was dangerously near to melting, however hard she tried to keep it intact. She wasn't ready for it, nor did she intend to let him know it. . . .

As if to confuse her more, Vince reverted to his most businesslike self. It was almost pleasant to work with him on his project, except that she couldn't rid herself of the suspicion that this couldn't last. But the project was taking shape, and despite the fact that Vince's notes were so muddled, he was clear in what he wanted to do with them. Between them they began to formulate the work into rough shape by the end of the week. And suddenly all the haphazard bits and pieces he'd collected seemed to take on a definite form.

"I'd say we make quite a formidable team." Vince stretched his arms after a particularly long stint. "Don't go all coy on me and deny it, Julia!"

"I wasn't going to," she replied. "I entirely agree with you—at least as far as work's concerned."

"Well, that's a change anyway." He moved over to a side table and poured them each a glass of sherry from a cut glass decanter. "I'd say we deserve a drink. We've both worked very hard this week and I hope the trip to Skye tomorrow will compensate a bit. It's a wild and beautiful island. It'll melt even your stony heart."

"Don't count on it. Anyway, I'm enjoying the work, so let's leave it at that, shall we?"

At least they were having a reasonably normal conversation, Julia thought. And she had to admit that when he wasn't being objectionable or arrogant, she admired him for his energy, his charisma, his determination. He was a relentless stickler for detail in his work, and besides that, she freely admitted that he was every woman's dream in many ways. . . . She realised she was staring at him, and that there was a little smile playing around his lips. Julia sipped her sherry quickly, knowing that the next thought to slip into her head would be that it would be so easy to forget everything and fall in love with him . . . forget Martin, who was becoming a sweet, hazy memory, incredible though it seemed; forget Isla, in whom Vince was supposed to be more than interested, according to Fern, something he'd never bothered to deny; forget all the other women he must have loved before her. . . . He was clearly expecting this moment to turn into one of deeper intimacy, but she found herself unable to smile back at him. If only he loved her. If she could be assured that he was free to do so, how different everything would be. As it was . . .

"I'm looking forward to visiting Skye," she said coolly. "It's certainly one of the perks of the job!"

His smile faded. "Good," he said curtly. "I suggest that you wear casual clothes—slacks, certainly. Part of the way to the old crofter's cottage will have to be done by pony. Does that worry you?"

Julia stared at him. "Well, I'm glad you warned me anyway." She began to wonder what she was letting herself in for.

He laughed mirthlessly. "We'll check into the hotel at Portree when we arrive and drive as far as we can across the island. But on the final stretch, there's no roadway for cars, so we've got no choice. I don't imagine you'd want to tramp two or three miles across soggy glens and burns on foot! So go prepared for getting muddy. I want to make an early start. We should get all our business done tomorrow, with luck, then we might have a couple of hours' sightseeing before we get the car ferry back to Kyle of Lochalsh the following day."

"Dunvegan Castle?" she said at once.

"So you remember the story Andrew told you of the Macleods' stronghold. Aye, we may get to see it and, if you're lucky, a little of its magic, but all of Skye has a magic quality. You'll know it when you see it."

He leaned toward her and for a second Julia thought he was going to kiss her. But he turned away abruptly, telling her she'd better get an early night as he wanted to be away at first light.

"Whatever time is that meant to be?" she exclaimed.

"Five o'clock in the morning," he said shortly. "Can you face it?"

"Of course. It's the only time to travel," she flung back. "Good-night then, Vince. I'd better go and pack, and I'll see you at five A.M!"

* * *

Once Julia had packed all she needed, she set her alarm clock for four A.M., giving a little groan as she did so, and tried to sleep. It was difficult, because she was excited about the coming trip . . . over the sea to Skye. She avoided thinking of all the time she and Vince would have alone together. She must have slept, because it seemed only seconds later that the alarm clock was ringing and she was glancing toward the window at a pale yellow dawn.

Vince tapped on her door a few minutes later, and she called out that she was awake. It was chilly, and she pulled a white woollen sweater over her head with a shiver, and over it a smoke-blue trouser suit. She packed an extra pair of slacks and a black sweater, but the jacket could do double duty. For the Friday evening at the hotel, she'd packed the flattering turquoise dress that Vince hadn't seen yet. . . .

He was in the dining room before her. Someone had been up early enough to prepare grapefruit and toast and hot coffee. But he told her they could stop for a more substantial breakfast if they needed it later on.

"This is fine," Julia told him. "I'm not used to eating at this time of day."

"Then as soon as we've finished, we'll be on our way," he said briefly.

She suddenly realised that Vince, too, had an air of anticipation about him. A boyish eagerness that was oddly endearing after his usual worldliness. *Careful*, she warned herself, *or you'll end up being besotted over him.* And the less prosaic part of her told her that that state wasn't so very far away anyway. . . .

They drove through the autumn morning, with the mist low over Loch Lomond and shrouding the hills in mystery. A pale pinky-yellow light streaked the dawn sky, and it was a weird and rather special feeling to realise they were almost the only two people speeding through the silent countryside, with nature only slowly waking up all around them. It was so ethereally beautiful, the spangled spiders' web on plants and bushes, the soft rustle of trees looming through the mist as if they, too, woke up with the coming of day; the long slow gleam of sunlight on water as the clouds of vapour began to disperse. Sharing such moments with a companion sensitive enough not to break them with words was precious.

The countryside had changed subtly. It had been splendid before but now, as range after range of mountains soared skyward, roads became mere tracks, and the silence enveloped them, it was awesome, spectacular, and very, very beautiful. There was something magical in seeing the dawn with someone you loved beside you. Julia swallowed convulsively, concentrating on the rugged grandeur of nature that could make you feel so insignificant and yet so very much a part of the pattern of things. For a second, she was almost tempted to blurt out her feelings to Vince, knowing instinctively that he'd understand, and that this would be one of the times when he wouldn't mock. But just as he, too, remained silent, drinking in the beauty of the morning, the words stayed deep inside her, too emotional to be spoken.

And then came the long drive through wild and eerie Glencoe, with its magnificent mountains and lonely passes, so aptly known as the Glen of Weeping after the massacre. Those old ghosts were no more than faint echoes on the breeze now, but Julia was glad when the glen was behind them and the picturesque town of Fort William came into view, at the foot of the giant granite mass of Ben Nevis, its humps and fissures bathed in sunshine and shadow.

They reached the little town of Kyle of Lochalsh in time to have coffee and scrambled eggs at a small café before boarding the car ferry across to Kyleakin, the nearest point of Skye to the mainland. It was so close Julia felt as if she could reach across and touch it, but there was still the heady feeling of crossing water even for so short a trip. And then they were driving off on to the island soil.

Almost as soon as they left the tiny coastal township behind, Julia realised that the road was climbing steadily. Skye had always held a fascination for her, with its romantic associations of Bonnie Prince Charlie and his traumatic journey, disguised as the maid of Flora MacDonald, over the sea to Skye.

The countryside was wild and rugged, with steep hills and plunging glens, and crystal-clear tumbling waterfalls that had a music of their own. Julia caught her breath as the great granite domes of the barren hills came into view . . . coloured a strange unearthly pink to give a weird moonscape appearance. At that moment, she could easily believe the two of them were alone on an alien planet. . . .

"I've never seen anything like it," she said in amazement.

"They're called the Red Hills," he told her. "There's some of the most spectacular scenery in Scotland on Skye, and much of it is steeped in history and folklore. It's incredible to think that some of the old crofters have never been to the mainland or seen television, even though they're relatively near to civilisation. In fact, the whole island is only fifty miles long, and you know how short a crossing it was by ferry."

"Not everyone wants or needs civilisation, I suppose," Julia murmured. The road to Portree bordered the rugged coastline and rose and dipped with startling changes in scenery.

There were small lochs no bigger than a village pond, but incredibly blue and calm, mirroring the cotton-wool clouds in their depths. There were whitewashed cottages with thatched roofs huddled on the hillsides, with the hardy sheep grazing nearby. Vince slowed the car as they neared the village of Broadford, pointing toward a mountain with a Gaelic name, Beinn na Caillich, some two miles westward.

"There's a large cairn on its peak, and beneath it are the remains of a Norwegian princess from the thirteenth century. It's said she wanted the winds of Norway to blow over her grave."

"How beautiful," Julia said softly. Vince's affinity with those old Norsemen was very strong, she realised. How could she ever have assumed him to be a shallow playboy? There was so much depth to his character, and suddenly she knew how glad and privileged she was to be sharing his project with him. She was already becoming immersed in the magic and myths of Skye, loving every minute of it, and finding it surprisingly easy to forget a way of life that was orderly and regimented.

Portree was a town of whitewashed houses at the mouth of a pretty loch. They arrived about midmorning and Julia was glad to stretch her legs and look about her. Vince indicated the small hotel where they would stay the night, and they went across to have some coffee and book rooms.

There was time to explore Portree a little before they started on the drive across the island to where the old crofter lived. The town was quaint but businesslike, with whitewashed houses and a harbour from where steamers made trips round the island and took tourists to the small Isle of Raasay. The sun was warm on their heads by now, and Vince suggested they buy fruit and rolls and cheese and canned drinks for a picnic lunch later. They would need refreshment when they had to leave the car and hire the ponies for the last trek across the glen to the crofter's cottage.

As Vince turned the car towards the minor road out of Portree that looked little more than a muddy track, Julia suddenly thought that if someone had told her a couple of weeks ago that she'd be sharing a picnic on Skye in the middle of nowhere with a man who alternately fascinated and infuriated her, she'd have said they were crazy.

The drive across the width of Skye was something to be remembered. It took less than half an hour, and yet in that short time the romance and mystery of the island's heritage was as vivid as if it were something tangible. The bubbling burns sang to them; the towering mountains sheltered them; long stretches of verdant green were like oases in terrain that grew steadily wilder, more rugged and brooding. It was easy to imagine it being a sanctuary for a prince who fled his homeland; easy to believe in magic and Norse sea-pirates and all things mystical. Skye wove an inexorable spell of enchantment around her. . . .

The twisting track came to an end at a lonely farm with a sign proclaiming Ponies For Hire that creaked in the wind as it swung to and fro. Was she crazy to be here? Julie wondered as she and Vince sat in the car eating cheese rolls and crisp green apples, and swilled the lot down with ice-cold lager like two mad tourists.

"Ready then?" He smiled at her. "Not going to chicken out on me, are you?"

"Of course not!" Just as long as he didn't realise how nervous she suddenly felt. Ahead of them lay nothing but a wild glen with towering cliffs and the sound of rushing water. . . .

"That's my girl." He leaned across and kissed her. "Come on, then. Let's go and hire some ponies."

The old crofter had given them directions, but even so it felt a little like stepping out into the unknown as the farmer shook his head slightly when Vince checked with him, and handed over the reins of two sturdy little ponies.

"It's Old Hamish ye're wanting, is it?" The farmer scratched his head as if only madmen would want the likes of Old Hamish. "Oh, aye, your directions are sound enough, but I doubt ye'll get much sense out o' that one."

He was still shaking his head after them as they started out. Two or three miles wasn't far, Julia told herself—not when you were in a car on solid main roads—but it was a different prospect with the ground under the pony's feet slippery and soggy, and the sky gradually darkening overhead with the threat of rain, and the hills seeming to change shape and colour as storm clouds raced across their faces, their protectiveness turning to a dark and brooding menace. . . .

"Are you all right?" Vince looked back at her from his leading position. "I don't think we're going to get a downpour, but in any case, we must be nearly there."

Thank goodness for that, she thought fervently. She wondered if she'd ever be able to walk again, and thought longingly of a bath at the hotel in Portree that evening. But as the first drops of rain splashed down in front of them they saw the welcome sight of the stone-built cottage and the curl of smoke from its chimney. It was directly beneath the shadow of a mountain, frail in its grandiose setting.

"Hamish Buckie's kingdom," Vince said solemnly. He dismounted and helped Julia down from her pony, then tied both to a gnarled tree trunk that had long since given up the struggle to grow. She felt suddenly nervous of this unknown crofter, but Vince smiled at her reassuringly, and knocked boldly at the door.

It was opened almost at once by a wizened, hardy little man with a wisp of grey hair on his head and more on his eyebrows. His eyes were bright and darting, his voice strong, considering he looked about eighty years old. His dialect was almost incomprehensible, half-Gaelic, half-Scots, but with an accent all his own.

He had been expecting them, and though the atmosphere in the cottage was almost fetid at first, Hamish had prepared three mugs on the bare table and an iron kettle boiled away merrily on the hearth over the wood fire. They were clearly to be entertained, and within minutes Julia was touched to see that, to Old Hamish, Vincent Galbraith was like royalty, and she, as his consort, almost the same.

It was hard to make verbal contact at first, but Vince brought out Hamish's scrawled letters to indicate that he was who he said he was. The old man waved them aside.

"Nae read," he announced. "Nae write. Farmer wrote yon screeds. Ye've the right look about ye. Old Hamish knows ye."

He might well be mad, Julia thought, but she suddenly realised how gently Vince was going about his business with the illiterate old man, asking his questions with infinite patience until Hamish stumped off to a cupboard in the wall and came back with a tin box.

There was a pile of old letters inside, some very old indeed, and Vince took them to the grimy window to study the faded writing. The old dog in a box by the hearth, who'd hardly moved his head when they arrived, and was probably as old as Hamish in canine terms, suddenly perked up as Julia idly stroked his head.

"He likes ye." Hamish nodded. "He misses *her*."

She gave a nod back. Who *her* was, she had no idea, but presumably a wife had once lived here in this wilderness. It was a chilling thought. Hamish didn't talk much. He'd probably lived alone so long he'd almost lost the art, Julia decided, though he looked across interestedly at Vince as he became absorbed in the contents of the tin box.

"Ye can have the box," he grunted. "It's nae use to me. Belonged to Graindfaither. . . ."

"I'll buy it, Mr. Buckie . . . Hamish," Vince said

hastily as the old man looked blank at the unexpected title.

"Buy it?" Hamish gave a cackling laugh. "What would I want wi' money out here? Farmer gi'es me all I want in return for jobs."

"A pony, then," Vince insisted. "To save you walking back and forth to the farm in bad weather."

Julia stared at him. Were there treasures in the box . . . ? Vince hadn't shown her, though she'd dearly like to have known. Hamish stared, too.

"We-ll. A pony now. Folks don't give such things away for nothin'," he said suspiciously.

"It's not for nothing," Vince told him. "A pony in exchange for the tin box, Hamish."

"Aye. Done. Ye can trust a Galbraith." The old man stretched out a gnarled hand and took Vince's tightly. It touched Julia to see the sudden spark of pride in Hamish's eyes.

"I'll arrange it with Farmer." Vince slipped easily into the old man's way of talking. They finished their tea and said they must start back before the weather changed. So far the rain had held off, but the sky was dark and the atmosphere oppressive. Before they left, Vince pulled out a tin of tobacco for the old man. Julia had had no idea he had it, but it was a sure bet that Hamish would smoke, and he took it with a deference due to his visitor. Only the finger tapping the forehead was missing, Julia thought. In this remote barren corner, the Galbraiths were obviously still held in great esteem by Old Hamish.

And by Farmer, too, she discovered, when they reached the farm again. Vince had hustled her back along the soggy track without giving her any explanation of his finds at Hamish Buckie's cottage. He'd show her everything later, he promised, but first he wanted to get back to the car. Julia was in agreement. This was suddenly a cold, menacing place to be, and they urged the ponies on as fast as they'd go. She saw the farm buildings with a sigh of relief, and Farmer came out at once to stable the ponies and to offer them oat cakes and whiskey. The few miles had seemed endless, and Julia knew her nerves were taut.

"We mustn't refuse or we'll offend him deeply," Vince muttered, and clearly the Farmer looked on Vince as some kind of god, and referred to him as Laird whenever he spoke to him. But the whiskey was so raw and strong it left Julia gasping, and she was forced to add double the quantity of water before she could get it down. Farmer had other business beside cows and sheep, she concluded! An illicit still probably made the winter nights less bleak. . . .

Vince was doing business with him very formally, and pound notes were changing hands. A great many of them, Julia saw with surprise. He'd come prepared for this.

"I want to purchase a pony for Old Hamish, Farmer. Let him have it next time he comes here to do his jobs, and I'm going to give you some money to buy him a few home comforts, food and a radio and whatever he needs. You'll see to it for me?"

"Aye, Laird, it'll be done at once."

"Good. You have my address. If you'll send me the receipts, that'll be good enough."

His kindness toward the old man was unexpected. All right, there might be things in the tin box that were worth a fortune, but as far as Hamish was concerned, Vince could have them and they'd be forgotten in a week. He didn't have to do any of this. . . . She felt a new respect for him, and for the businesslike way he asked Farmer to send receipts, which was exactly the right way to go about things.

They left the farm just before five o'clock, and once out of sight and bumping along the narrow winding track in the car, Julia turned to Vince.

"I'm bursting to know what you found! And, Vince—I'm touched by what you did for that old man. It must be terrible to live like that. . . ."

"Not to him," he said briefly. "He'd be petrified in a town. But he's owed something, if only for the years of service his ancestors gave to our family. As to the tin box . . . I can't be sure, but a pony and a good meal in his stomach is a poor reward for it."

He pulled the car to a stop and switched off the engine. The tin box was quite large and a bit rusty. It contained old letters crammed inside older envelopes, a few barely legible documents, some old coins that might be worth investigating; a piece of tattered and faded tartan that was indistinguishable but must have meant something to somebody for it to be saved, and several brooches.

Vince picked up one of them and rubbed at the dirt and grime on it. It was circular, quite ornate, with a narrow sword crossing the hollow centre. He handed it to Julia. She felt the old excitement inside her, the way it used to be when she and Mr. Pollard discovered something unexpectedly.

"It's absolutely filthy," she murmured. "But it's copper, isn't it? And pretty old, though not ancient. Maybe eighteenth century. . . . I don't think I'd place it any older, but we'll be able to judge better when it's cleaned."

"And this?" He handed her the next piece without saying any more.

It was caked with dirt as well, but this time the adrenaline was racing through her as she held the piece in her hands. It was larger than the other piece, also circular, but made of silver. She imagined how it would originally have looked, glowing richly with its intricate, deeply engraved design of leaves and interlacing, but the interlacing stretched right across the centre gap and was caught with a jewel. It was dulled and grimy now, but it looked very much like . . .

"It's an emerald," she gasped. "Not the most perfect, perhaps, but this brooch must be worth a great deal of money. I've never seen anything quite like it, Vince."

"I have," he told her. "It's an annular brooch with which the plaid was fastened to the shoulder. They used to be worn by women as a betrothal brooch. Sometimes they passed them back to their men as a lucky token in battle. But this is certainly a rarity."

"And paid for by a pony and a few luxuries for an old man. . . ."

She wasn't meaning to criticise, and if Vince had offered a fine house on the mainland she knew instinctively that Old Hamish would have refused at once. He'd given the best payment he could have made. She gave a sudden shiver as a roll of thunder echoed round the hills at that moment. Vince took the brooch out of her hand and replaced it in the tin box with the rest of the items.

"They were also supposed to keep away witches, but I don't know about the gods being angry at taking the brooch away from the island," he commented as the thunder almost shook the air, and a sudden lashing of rain struck the car. "I think we'd better get safely to Portree and back to reality again."

They spoke very little as Vince negotiated the narrow road, which was quickly turning into a quagmire. Every now and then lightning zigzagged in front of them. Julia was almost limp with relief when the little town came into sight and they could make a dash from the car to the hotel. There was no time then to do any more than have a quick bath and change clothes before they were summoned by a loud gong for dinner.

Julia felt terribly tired. Remembering how long they had been up that day, it was no wonder. All that and the excitement of the tin box, and the hair-raising journey back to Portree . . . She was too tired even to contemplate the value of the annular brooch. They would take it to Aberdeen with them, Vince told her, where there was an expert on ancient Highland jewellery, and have it properly cleaned and valued.

"Though as far as I'm concerned, it's priceless," he said.

The day had taken its toll of Vince, too, she realised. He looked tired, the arrogant look softened and mellowed with both excitement and weariness. There was a look of strain around his mouth, and she felt a sudden urge to smooth it away with her fingers.

She concentrated on her meal, which was good and tasty. Vince was away somewhere in a world of his own, somewhere with his Celtic ancestors, and she felt suddenly shut out. And she knew without any doubt how much she wanted to be part of his world. To be part of him . . . She knew without any doubt how much she loved him. . . .

"I think I'll go straight to bed after dinner," she murmured. She didn't look at him, because he'd surely see all there was to see in her eyes, and she knew that tonight wasn't the time. . . . He sounded almost relieved when he said he'd do the same once he'd had a last tot of whiskey to keep out the cold. But Julia's head was still swimming from Farmer's raw brew, and she climbed the stairs to her bedroom, almost too tired to undress.

Outside, the thunder still exploded around the hills and lightning lit the austere little room from time to time. The rain was coming down in a furious torrent, and Julia suddenly shivered, remembering Vince's teasing remark about the gods being angry at the brooch being taken off the island. It was all nonsense, of course, but somehow, on this ancient island, nothing was too fanciful to believe. Especially when you were alone . . .

Julia closed her eyes tightly as a violent crash of thunder seemed to crack right overhead. She wasn't normally frightened of it, but this lot seemed to be directed right on this very hotel—and she didn't want to be alone. She wanted Vince; she wanted the door to open and for him to come storming in and gather her up in his arms, holding her and loving her. Even if it meant nothing to him, except for the moment, she wanted his love . . . but he didn't appear, and whatever she had half-expected of this night, she spent it curled up alone and disappointed, and finally fell exhausted into a dreamless sleep.

Chapter Eight

To Julia's relief, the storm had spent itself during the night, and the morning was cool and calm. Short though the crossing to the mainland was, she didn't fancy being buffeted about by strong winds and surging seas.

"I'm afraid there's no point in our going up to Dunvegan," Vince told her at breakfast. "The castle's not open on weekends, and as we have a fair journey ahead of us, I suggest we start back as soon as we're ready."

She had no objections. She was so tired she felt she could sleep for a week, and Vince seemed too preoccupied to be very interested in tourism anyway. It was a pity about Dunvegan, but maybe some other time. . . .

She dozed in the car as it sped over the miles back to Galbraith Hall, hardly noticing the picturesque villages and lonely glens and mountains. All she wanted was to sleep and sleep; her legs were stiff and she had a crick in her neck, but Vince was smiling at her quite amicably as he reached for the tin box and their luggage on their arrival home.

"Come on, sleepyhead," he said. "I don't know how your head feels, but my shoulder's sore where you've been leaning against it."

132

She hadn't realised, and she felt her face redden at the thought. She was still very aware of the way her emotions had overtaken her last night, when she had wanted him so badly, but she was very glad now that he hadn't tried anything at the hotel. To ache for someone because you loved them was one thing . . . but the way he looked when he told her he wanted her was something else. Without love it was meaningless, and it was even worse when all the loving was on one side only. . . .

"Vince! I thought you'd be here when I got home last night!"

Fern's petulant voice sounded right beside the car, and Julia remembered that she was coming home to have her fitting with Isla for the games. The girl was clearly put out that Vince should have been away, and as he hauled his long legs out of the car, Fern clung to his arm, ignoring Julia completely.

"Haven't you forgotten your manners?" he asked her. He opened Julia's door for her and she got out stiffly. She'd rather he hadn't pulled Fern up, because she only looked sulky and muttered hello.

"Are you taking me into Glasgow this afternoon?" Fern demanded. "Rose said Thoms might have to take me, but now you're here, you will, won't you? Isla will want to see you."

"Maybe. We're both exhausted, but we had a very worthwhile trip. I may tell you about it if you're good."

"Oh, that old man you were going to see." Fern wrinkled her nose as they all went indoors. "I don't like old things. They smell."

Perversely, Julia didn't want Vince to show anyone else the contents of the tin box. Until now, the excitement still belonged to the two of them. She knew that couldn't last, and that Rose and the children had more right to them than she did. The utter depression of weariness was overtaking her very fast.

But first she had to phone Andrew to say she was too tired to be good company that evening after all, and to postpone their date. In fact, what she really needed was to unwind in Aunt Meg's good solid company, and when she'd got it sorted out with Andrew she'd phone her aunt and suggest going back to stay at Strathrowan overnight. Aunt Meg would be fascinated to hear about the trip to Skye.

An hour later, she'd bathed and washed her hair and partly dried it so that it curled damply on her shoulders. She wore a warm bronze-coloured sweater and the cream-coloured slacks, and unpacked her small case, repacking it for Aunt Meg's. The turquoise dress was hung in her wardrobe with the rueful thought that Vince hadn't even commented on it last night, which proved that he must have been miles away from her in spirit. She made her phone calls and felt warmed by her aunt's eagerness to see her again and hear all her news.

But there was one piece of news she wasn't going to hear, Julia thought. She held an imaginary conversation with herself.

". . . yes, it was wonderful on Skye . . . mysterious and magical, as Vince promised. Only for me, the magic would be anywhere as long as he was there . . . and did I tell you that I love him . . . totally, madly and forever . . . ?"

The tap on her door made her almost drop the comb with which she was untangling her hair. She opened it to find Vince standing there unsmilingly.

"Lunch will be ready in ten minutes," he said. He came inside, closing the door. Julia felt her heartbeats quicken again, but it was clear he had something special to say.

"While you were sleeping in the car, I decided it would be best to keep the contents of Hamish's box to ourselves until it has all been verified in Aberdeen."

Julia nodded. "Naturally I'll say nothing about it.

I wouldn't have done so anyway. Discretion is part of the job, Vince." She was slightly annoyed that he thought she might have blabbed everything in a burst of excitement as if she was as gauche as Fern.

"Oh—and Vince," she added, "if you're going to Glasgow with Fern tonight, would you mind dropping me off at Aunt Meg's? I've arranged to stay there tonight."

Her eyes dared him to make any comment, but she might have known it would be more than he could resist. There was a sudden gleam in his mocking dark eyes.

"What happened to the plans for Andrew then? I thought the young lover was expecting you tonight!"

"Let's just say I feel the need of some relaxing company tonight, and Aunt Meg fills the bill better than any male could," she said wearily. "Incredible though it may seem to you, even the most appealing men can get a little wearing at times, and that's no reflection on Andrew, either!"

She should have known Vince would immediately take her comment as being personal to him instead.

"If you're finding my company and the work too much, I've already said you should tell me. But you can hardly expect me to curb my enthusiasm at such exciting and unexpected finds." His voice was curt and reproving.

"Of course the work isn't too much," she snapped. "And I'm as thrilled as you at the things we discovered. I must admit, I do feel very tired just at the moment, though, I assure you, I'm not some little hothouse flower—" Julia bit her lip, knowing she was saying too much. Anyway, his word for her was just the opposite, she thought suddenly. Ice-maiden . . . but she had never felt less like that. She was wilting by the minute from sheer fatigue. The comb fell from her fingers, and as she went to pick it up to start dragging it nervously through her long hair again, it was Vince who retrieved it.

"You look all in. Turn round," he said abruptly.

She did so automatically, and seconds later she felt him draw the wide-toothed comb down the length of her hair. It was such an unexpectedly intimate act that it was almost unbearable to Julia, and she felt the salt sting of tears behind her eyelids. The little performance didn't last long. After a few minutes, she heard Vince give a muttered exclamation and fling the comb on the bed as he twisted her toward him in his arms.

"Why must we keep up this stupid battle?" he asked angrily.

"You know why!" Because of Isla. . . . The words hung on her lips, but before she could utter them he had pulled her roughly toward him and then he was kissing her eyes, her cheeks, her lips . . . stunning her into submission with his overpowering desire.

"I only know I want you more than I've wanted any woman in my life." He spoke thickly against her throat. "Right now you smell of fresh herbs and springtime, and you drive me wild."

His hands were seeking her breasts, and his knee was forcing hers apart. His demanding maleness was making her weak, and she found herself arching against him with the sweet ache of longing that his touch aroused so relentlessly. His kisses were urgent on her mouth as she was crushed against him. She could feel the tautness of his thigh muscles and the thudding of his heart next to hers. With every particle of her, she wanted him as much as he wanted her. Her head swam with the dizziness of desire. . . .

"We missed a golden opportunity last night, my lovely Julia," she heard him say raggedly against her soft skin.

Suddenly Julia came to her senses. An opportunity . . . was that how he saw their being together . . . nothing more than that? It denigrated all the love that was burning inside her for him. She wept inside at the injustice of it all, that all he could think about was lost opportunity when what she craved was his tender and exclusive love. . . . She hardly realised she was struggling to get out of his embrace until she saw the anger sparkling in his eyes, but before he could force her to submit totally, the door of the bedroom burst open and Fern stood there.

She looked from one to the other of them, still clasped in each other's arms in what looked like a very intimate embrace, and her face went a brilliant, furious red. Despite her mature act, she was still very much a child at that moment.

"I came to get you for lunch, Vince," she said shrilly.

"You could try knocking on a guest's door," he snapped. "Haven't you any manners—"

"I wonder what Isla would say if she knew you were so familiar with Julia's bedroom?"

Vince let go of Julia so suddenly she nearly fell. "What do I care what Isla thinks? You seem to be obsessed by Isla, but for your information, Isla and I understand each other perfectly, and you, young lady, have got a lot to learn about grownups! Now get out of here and tell Rose I'm on my way."

He glanced at Julia. "You'll have to come down with damp hair. Rose hates to be kept waiting."

He almost pushed his sister out of the room. Julia stared after them both with burning eyes. It didn't matter who was on the receiving end of his anger, they all got the same treatment. He just couldn't tolerate people who opposed his plans in any way. *He* was the intolerable one, if he only realised it. But what Julia could hardly credit was his remark about Isla. After Fern's taunt, he'd certainly shown his ruthlessness in getting his own way, even total disregard for his girlfriend's feelings was within his grasp. Or did this "perfect understanding" he spoke about include her turning a blind eye to his little indiscretions . . . ?

Julia sat down heavily on the bed for a few minutes. So many of her encounters with Vince seemed to end up this way, leaving her drained, wilted, totally bewildered. She pulled herself together with an effort, remembering that Rose was expecting her downstairs, and didn't like to be kept waiting. . . . And if it hadn't been for Fern coming up to fetch them for lunch . . .

The other emotions that had held her so exquisitely captive seconds before Fern burst into the room still lingered. Despite her anger because Vince could play around with two women's feelings so shamelessly, she had to admit that those moments when her senses had soared to dizzy heights had been the sweetest she had ever known. She had been almost ready to forget all about convention then . . . as she had been in the little hotel in Portree when Vince hadn't come to her, and she had wanted him so much. Wanted him with an urgency that was almost shameful. . . .

"Blast him," Julia whispered now. "I should never have left Cornwall to come here. I should have stayed where I belong."

With memories of a love she'd thought was to last a lifetime. Now she knew that hearts could not only be mended, but break all over again. It just wasn't worth it, she thought tremulously. She closed her eyes, and instantly she was imagining Vince's arms holding her, and she asked herself just who was she kidding?

She got up quickly and went down to lunch, hoping she appeared reasonably calm. It was obvious to her, at least, that Vince had told Fern a few home-truths, for the girl was rude and sullen to everyone. A finishing school in Switzerland would have its work cut out with that one, Julia thought.

Rose just ignored her, used to her moods and knowing she was best left alone. Anyway, she was more interested in knowing the outcome of the visit to Skye.

"Will you tell me, Julia, since Vince is being so obstinate?" She turned to Julia in smiling exasperation.

"I'm sure you don't really expect me to do that, Mrs. Galbraith." Julia was the perfect discreet assistant, smiling artlessly back. "I don't want to be thrown out on my ear just yet, and Vince will tell you everything when he's ready."

Vince wasn't so gentle. "Just leave it, Rose. You'll know it all in good time."

Rose looked at each of them, suddenly aware of the tension between them.

"I see you made a good choice of assistant," she said mildly.

"And don't think you can pump her while I'm taking Fern to Glasgow, because she's going to Meggie's until tomorrow. I know you when you start getting persuasive and turning on the charm."

Like mother, like son . . .

"And you'll be seeing Isla, no doubt?" Rose went on.

"That's right. Has anyone got any comments to make about that?" He looked keenly at Fern, and his mother gave a short laugh.

"My goodness, you're spiky tonight, Vince. Well, I'm not sorry you're all going out if I'm to get no more out of you. I shall relax in the garden and enjoy my own company. At least I'll have no one to snap at me!"

As soon as lunch was over the three of them set off in one of the bigger family cars. Fern sat stonily throughout the journey. Julia was highly thankful, when Vince stopped the car at her aunt's cottage, to get away from the stormy-faced Galbraiths.

"I'll find my own way back to the Hall tomorrow

evening," she said as she climbed out of the passenger seat.

"Don't be ridiculous," Vince said coldly. "I'll fetch you."

He pulled the door shut and was gone before she could argue or ask about time. He was the most infuriating man, she fumed. And yet she watched the car drive away with an odd mixture of relief and loneliness, and knew to her annoyance that it was spiced with a dash of jealousy, too, because Vince was seeing Isla that evening. She turned quickly to go into her aunt's cottage. It seemed incredible to think she'd hardly known Vince Galbraith the last time she stepped through the cottage door. It felt as if she'd known him a lifetime. It happened like that with some people.

Aunt Meg had the kettle and the tea already in the pot. Within ten minutes they were busily talking as if Julia had never been away, and the relaxation was wonderful.

"Tell me what you thought of Skye," Aunt Meg said eagerly. "Do you know, I've never been there?"

"It's the most beautiful place," Julia told her. "And awesome, as well, with the wild mountains and deep glens. It's an island I'll never forget." She pushed away the memory of the lonely night when all she'd wanted was to feel Vince's arms holding her tight.

"What about the old man Vince went to see? Was he as dour as you'd have expected?"

Julia smiled. "He was rather sweet, really, though very difficult to understand. A bit like someone from another world. I shouldn't think he'd know what to do with a telephone if he saw one!"

"He'd be no good for me, then!" Aunt Meg said with a laugh in her voice.

"I didn't think you were in the market for marriage."

"That I'm not, but if I was forty years younger I might be setting my sights on Vince Galbraith." She chuckled, and didn't miss the pursing of Julia's soft mouth. "Been playing you up a bit, has he?" she added shrewdly.

"Oh, he can be so—so impossible sometimes," Julia burst out. She hadn't intended making any remarks about him at all, but her aunt nodded in agreement. "And so—so—"

"Sexy?" she said wickedly, and then laughed at Julia's look. "Come on, love, I may be old, but I'm not blind! What that young man needs is a wife who's as strong-willed as himself."

"Such as Isla Macleod?" The name sprang into Julia's mind at once. Nobody could say she wasn't strong-willed, besides being glamorous and ambitious and socially acceptable. "I'd like to forget about Vince Galbraith for the time being, if you don't mind," she said distantly.

Not that that was likely, but she had no intention of wearing her heart on her sleeve. Her aunt changed the subject at once. Privately, she wasn't too displeased that Julia and Vince had apparently clashed right off. At least it had taken the bleak look out of Julia's beautiful eyes, the look that had been so evident when she had arrived at Strathrowan. And there was that old Shakespearean quotation . . . methinks the lady doth protest too much . . . but she kept her thoughts to herself for the time being.

It seemed no time at all until the day was over, and Sunday was spent at kirk in the morning and walking the hills in the afternoon. The days were cooling now, and there wouldn't be too many more like this, Julia thought sadly. The gorse still bloomed profusely. The kissing time . . . The thought was just a sweet memory now, and Martin a memory still dear in her heart, but no longer so painful to remember. At about seven clock Vince's two-seater roared up outside the cottage to collect her.

"We'll be seeing you in two weeks' time, Meggie," Vince told her. "The games, don't forget. Will your old heap get to the Hall by nine in the morning, or do you want Thoms to come and fetch you?"

"My Ford will go on for a good few years yet, my lad," Meg said in a sprightly voice. "The same as me!"

Vince laughed, giving her a squeeze as he said good-bye. Julia waved until the cottage was out of sight, and settled back in her seat. She was suddenly tongue-tied, even though she'd been rehearsing what she had to say to him.

"Straight home, or do you fancy a drink somewhere?" Vince said after a few minutes' silence.

"Straight home, but perhaps you could pull in somewhere on the way. I want to talk to you, Vince."

"Sounds ominous."

He drew the car to a halt in one of the grass verges that were viewing points above the loch. The sun was low in the sky, spreading pink fingers across the silvery waters of Loch Lomond. The sky was a poem in mauves and pinks. It was an evening made for lovers. . . .

"Fire away." He swivelled round in his seat to face her. She wished he wouldn't. She wished now she'd said it all while he was driving. She purposefully kept her eyes straight ahead of her.

"I can't go on the way we are, Vince," she said evenly. "I don't know what it is you want from me, but all I want is a working arrangement and nothing more. I've tried to make that clear, but now it has to be more definite. If you don't stop . . . pestering me, I shall leave Galbraith Hall."

She could hear her heart hammering in the silence. She knew without turning her head that he was furiously angry, that his face would be set in that cold, arrogant way of his, the dark eyes like black coals. She felt his hand grip her shoulder so hard she almost cried out, and she was forced to look into his face as he pulled her toward him.

"Pestering you!" he snapped coldly. "Is that what you think I've been doing? That reduces it to something rather cheap, wouldn't you say?"

"Maybe it is—to me," she whipped back. Wouldn't any girl feel the same, when she knew very well he was just playing with her emotions when it suited him? When Isla wasn't around . . .

He let her go suddenly and reached forward to restart the car. It roared into life, but she could still hear the rage in his voice.

"You needn't worry any longer, Miss Chase. From now on, our relationship will be purely professional. I've no wish to dispense with your services, because they're invaluable to me, but I most certainly won't force my unwelcome attentions on you again.

"As for what I want from you—I pity any man who thinks there's a woman's heart beneath those enticing curves. There's nothing but a lump of ice!"

The car tore round corners at breakneck speed, and Julia clung to the edge of her seat. "I wasn't aware that being 'nice' to the boss was part of the job." She put an emphasis on the word that he couldn't mistake. "It certainly wasn't included in my last job—"

"From what you've told me, your last boss was as ancient as his goods," Vince said coldly. "Is that the only type of man you feel comfortable around? I'd like to know just what happened in your life that's made you so afraid of a normal relationship with a man."

She cringed in her seat. She wasn't going to give him the satisfaction of knowing how heartbreakingly close he was to the truth. She hadn't even realised Martin's death had affected her in that way until

Vince Galbraith had begun his assault on her senses. As always, she took refuge in anger.

"Can't you get it into your head even now that it's your—your arrogance I object to?" she stormed at him. "You expect every woman to be eager and willing to give in to you. I'd have thought you might have been satisfied with Isla. She's such a perfect match for you, in more ways than one—and it would certainly please your dear sister!"

"Leave my sister out of it. She's only a child," he snapped. "As for Isla—we go back a long time, but I wasn't aware it was Isla we were discussing—"

"Maybe it's time we did," Julia snapped back. "I don't doubt that she's pretty generous with her favours—"

"Yes, she is, as a matter of fact, Isla's all woman, which is something you seem to have forgotten how to be. But as long as you give me complete satisfaction as my assistant, I'll ask nothing more from you from now on. You can rest assured of that."

The car jerked to a halt outside the Hall. Julia wished she could be sure he meant what he said, but she'd heard it too often before to be convinced. She climbed out of the car with shaking legs and walked ahead of him, refusing his offer to carry her overnight case. She'd done what she set out to do, but it hadn't given her much peace of mind.

Over the next two weeks she discovered another facet of Vince's character, and that was his iron self-control. When he made up his mind to something, he followed it through, and his latest ploy was to be coolly formal toward Julia, neither driving her too hard during working hours nor suggesting they go out together at other times. It unnerved her. She knew he was seeing Isla regularly. If he didn't tell her himself, then Rose did, as if there was a kind of conspiracy between them.

She should be relieved that he was leaving her

alone, but she wasn't. She knew she'd brought it all on herself. She'd made it clear that there was nothing doing between them because of Vince's involvement with Isla. But Julia was discovering something about herself, too. She didn't like to lose, and in that respect she and Vince were very much alike.

At least Fern wasn't around the place with her scowling face to add to the tension. She and James were to arrive at the Hall the night before the games, and go back to their respective schools again on the Sunday after. Julia had to admit that the less she saw of that little madam, the better she liked it.

"I've had some replies to my correspondence in Aberdeen," Vince told her on the Friday before the games. "There are a couple of people to see as well as the original plan for going through the archives. Though Old Hamish's box takes preference now. I suggest we go on Tuesday morning and get as much done as possible in the afternoon, stay overnight and go to the archives on Wednesday. We'll just stay the one night. I trust you've no objections?"

"Of course not. You're the boss," she murmured.

"I'll book us in at a large commercial hotel where I've stayed before." His voice was brisk. "It's rather an impersonal place, but I'm sure that will suit you fine."

In other words, he was telling her quite clearly that, as far as he was concerned, she was just Miss Julia Chase, assistant, and about as desirable as the wallpaper. It was just what she wanted . . . wasn't it? Except that she still loved him, and it was as much as she could do not to throw herself into his arms and beg him not to look at her so coldly, that she hadn't meant those things she'd said . . . that he could have what he wanted of her. . . .

But always, at the back of her mind, was Isla. And the fact that Vince Galbraith didn't seem to know the meaning of love. All he was interested in was one thing. And if she gave in to him on that and then he turned away from her, the heartache would begin all over again. She couldn't take the risk.

Fern and James arrived home that night, and Fern gave the family a preview of her outfit, parading in front of them all. Apart from her sullen expression, she really looked very good in her role of highland dancer, from the pert tam-o'-shanter to the black pumps on her feet. The kilt swirled in perfect pleats as she spun round in a circle, arms above her head with fingertips touching, the silk blouse fitting nicely on her slight figure.

Whatever she lacked in good manners, she made up for in poise, Julia admitted. But the finishing school in Switzerland might be a good idea; for all her worldly self-possession, Fern was a very introverted child. Maybe, in getting away from the formidable Galbraith family and the constraints of a rigid boarding school, she would develop her own personality. It probably wasn't easy, knowing she was one of Rose's "after-thoughts." Not that it seemed to bother James a great deal. She heard him complaining now that dinner was ready, and he was fed up with watching Fern's performance. Predictably, Fern flounced off to change into jeans and T-shirt before joining them all in the dining room.

Aunt Meg arrived early the next morning. Vince was driving them both to the village high in the hills, and Thoms took Rose and the children in the family car. The day was fine and warm, and Julia felt a surge of anticipation at the prospect of seeing something new to her, but as traditional a part of Scotland's heritage as the tartan.

And it was everything she'd imagined. The little highland village was filled with a special kind of magic for the day. Surrounded by the majestic mountains, it was basically a one-street village with outlying farms, and one of the farms held the honour of providing the field this year. All the apparatus had been set up, and markers put in for the various pitches. The field was squared off by ropes so the spectators could stand all the way round. At one end was a presentation stand for Rose, her party, and the other V.I.P.'s. Another dais had pride of place for the Scottish dancing.

The games started early, with shotputting and caber-tossing. They went on all day, and Aunt Meg nudged Julia as the pipers began their practising, and she realised what it meant to have a score of different tunes being played at the same time. The teams of girls for the dancing disappeared, chattering, into the makeshift changing hut, and emerged later, transformed into groups of elegant young ladies with music in their hearts and magic in their feet.

She really did have style, Julia thought, as Fern pirouetted with the others on the dais. Her team won easily, and Fern stepped on to the dais as the head of the team to receive the cup from her mother on behalf of her school. She looked flushed and quite pretty, for once without the scowl that usually marred her features.

By midafternoon, Isla and Andrew had arrived at the village, presumably having left the shop in the hands of the assistants, and Julia didn't miss the way Isla came straight to the V.I.P. stand, to be given Vince's seat at once. It galled her to see the way everyone fussed over the other woman. As if she was one of the Galbraiths already, the thought struck her. Or about to be.

She turned away from them deliberately, giving Andrew a dazzling smile.

"Just in time for the pipers." He gave a mock groan as he whispered in her ear.

"I thought Scotsmen were supposed to love them," she whispered back.

"That's just a rumour we put about to keep the sassenachs out." They laughed together at his words, and to the others it must have looked as if they were on very good terms. She certainly hoped Vince thought so, and realised there were other men in the world besides himself who were attractive to women. Gentler men, like Andrew, who didn't try to blaze through her self-control with a ruthless passion that both exhilarated and stunned her.

The plaintive music of the bagpipes was filling the air now, in the final part of the competition, and suddenly Julia's heart leapt as she recognised the tune that was being played by the winner. "The Lovers' Lament." The tune Vince had played on that first night at Galbraith Hall, when she'd learned about the legend of the two lovers . . . and James's solemn voice had said that only those in love could hear the music. . . .

A force stronger than anything she'd known made her turn her head to where Vince was gazing toward her, as if compelling her to look into his dark, brooding eyes. It was a moment out of time, when no one else existed for either of them. It was a look of primeval desire, electrifying the air between them. A look that told her there was nothing on this earth that could keep them apart if he wanted her—and he did want her. . . .

Julia gave a sudden shiver as the music ended and a roar of applause greeted the piper. Andrew leaned toward her and took off his jacket to put round her shoulders, thinking she was cold. The movement blocked her from Vince's gaze, to her intense relief.

But it wasn't the cold that had sent the shiver running through her. It was more like a fever that gripped her . . . a fever that she knew only too well was a match for Vince Galbraith's, that would consume her totally if she didn't get away from it soon. . . .

Chapter Nine

When all the presentations were over, Julia discovered that there was to be an informal little get-together at the Hall, which included her Aunt Meg, and the Macleods, of course. Meals during the day had been picnic-style, but quite substantial, with hot pasties and plenty of coffee and cold snacks, so no one felt the need of a main meal.

Julia was glad when some of them started to leave the Hall. A day in the open air was tiring, particularly because she had been concentrating on so many different activities, absorbing though they had been. Aunt Meg drove off in the sputtering Ford around ten o'clock, and by then Julia was ready to drop into bed herself, but she felt obliged to stay up until the last of the visitors, Isla and her brother, of course, had gone.

Isla and Vince seemed to be having a prolonged good-bye outside, Julia suddenly realised with a stab of jealousy. And she forced herself to agree to seeing Andrew when she got back from Aberdeen sometime in the next week.

"Don't leave it too long." He grinned. "I'll start to think you don't like me or something!"

"Of course I like you." She hugged his arm. How

could anybody help liking him? But that was all it would ever be, however much he might want it otherwise, and she knew it. She reached up and kissed him on the lips, a light, friendly kiss given on the spur of the moment. But Andrew couldn't leave it like that. He grabbed her to him and kissed her with sudden enthusiasm, and when she broke away laughingly, she saw that Isla and Vince were standing just inside the doorway waiting for Andrew to fetch the car. Isla's eyes were uninterested, but Vince's were like chips of ice.

Now he probably thought she was more interested in Andrew than in himself, and that would be a blow to his ego, she fumed. Or he'd think she was just flirting with both of them, as the mood took her. She wished she didn't care what he thought, but she did.

"I'll be in touch next week," Andrew said in her ear, making the situation worse. She nodded, ignoring Vince completely as she said good-night to both the Macleods. By the time Vince came back inside the house she had gone up to bed.

On Monday afternoon there was a phone call from Aberdeen. Vince took it in the study while they were working, and she could tell by his voice that something was in the wind. He replaced the receiver carefully.

"That was Duncan Spragg. He's the specialist in ancient jewellery I told you about. We're to see him at four o'clock tomorrow afternoon. What I didn't tell you was that I sent the annular brooch to him a week ago and he's had it cleaned and inspected, so that we didn't have to wait on tenterhooks after we'd shown it to him. Thoms delivered it a week ago."

"And . . . ?" she demanded. "Don't keep me in suspense, Vince!"

He laughed. "He didn't say much, just that it's a find, and it's best that he discusses its value with me in person rather than on the phone. He wanted me to know that we weren't going to have a wasted journey, that's all."

His eyes glowed, and Julia knew how important the phone call had been. And it wouldn't be just for the value of the brooch. She knew Vince well enough now to know that it was far more than that. It was a link with the past of which he was so much a part, and she could understand his excitement.

"Vince, I'm so glad for you," she said sincerely.

For a moment all the conflict between them was gone, and his strong, angular face softened as he returned her smile. She caught her breath. That smile had been so rare lately, she had almost forgotten the impact it could have on her. He moved slowly toward her with his casual animal grace, and his hands were suddenly firm on her shoulders. Julia felt unable to move away.

"For *us,*" he said roughly. "You've got a stake in this venture, too."

She felt his fingers travel slowly down the length of her arms and a small shiver ran through her. Any semblance of tenderness from him would always have the power to make her feel weak, she thought. She tried to sound unaffected by his touch.

"Well, as your assistant, I suppose you could say that."

His eyes seemed to be boring into hers, as if they tried to read everything she was so determined to keep hidden from him.

"And is that the only way you see yourself—as my assistant?"

This was dangerous ground. Julia knew it, but she was still unwilling to move away from those softly moving fingers caressing her skin.

"What else? It's what I'm paid to be. If I get a little enthusiastic sometimes, it's because I'm doing the work I love. I told you that."

"Is it just the work you love?" he demanded.

"Vince, we aren't going to start all that again, are

we?" she asked unsteadily. She'd just about managed to subdue the memories of how he could storm his way through her defences. . . .

"Did we ever stop?" He was his old arrogant self again. "We're still the same two people, Julia. You're a very desirable young woman, and I don't think my masculinity has ever been in question!"

He could say that again, she thought weakly. He was moulding his body to hers now, and before she could say another word his lips were brushing hers with that tantalising softness that was so erotically awakening. Her hands felt damp as a tingling reaction raced through her veins.

"Please, Vince," she whispered. "Don't do this—"

"Then tell me again that it's only the work you love—if you can." He spoke with seductive urgency as his lips moved downward to her throat, and then lower, seeking the swell of her breasts inside her thin blouse.

The physical nearness of him was nearly knocking her resolution to bits. Why should she resist? Why not grasp at a little happiness? If only she wasn't so sure that disillusion would follow . . . that once he'd proven she was no longer the one woman who'd resisted all his charms, he'd leave her flat. She couldn't bear that. And she realised something else, too.

He'd been playing a game with her all this time, pretending to be cool and businesslike as she'd demanded, so that when he decided to turn on the charm again and start the big seduction scene, she'd be only too eager to fall for it. He'd probably planned all this with the precision of an army manoeuvre, and she wasn't going to let him get away with it. She remembered how he hated to be laughed at or teased. . . .

"All right, I'm telling you just that!" She hoped she sounded amused enough to fool him. "It's the work I love—that, and the chance to live in the style to which I'd like to become accustomed, of course. Isn't that what they say? It's not every day a working girl has such a chance offered to her. I'm not such an idiot as to turn all that down, even if it does mean putting up with *other* things."

She felt the tightness in her throat as his eyes lost their sparkle. If she hadn't known him better, she'd have believed he had been hurt by the way she'd just spoken. Maybe it was just that the idea that she could be ambitious had never really occurred to him. That, in looking for her next job, a reference with the impressive Galbraith Hall imprint on the letter heading . . . well, let him think it, and believe it. Let him get back to his glamourous Isla. Maybe *she* could cope with his roving eye, but it was something Julia couldn't, and wouldn't, stand. When she gave her own heart, it was totally and exclusively, and she expected nothing less in return.

He had let go of her now, standing barely a few inches from her, and yet they were suddenly worlds apart.

"I don't believe you'," he said coldly. "But have it your way—for now. It's impossible to talk sense with you when you're in this mood, so go and get your things packed for tomorrow. And don't forget that little turquoise dress!"

He banged out of the study, leaving her staring after him. *She* was impossible and moody? she raged . . . and then his last words penetrated. So he had noticed the turquoise dress after all! She was tempted to leave it behind, but she knew very well that she wouldn't.

She gave a long sigh. The job was the important thing now, she reminded herself, and it was a waste of energy to worry over Vince's insults. Instead, she would give all her attention to tomorrow, and a shiver of excitement ran through her at the prospect. The highlight of the trip would definitely be the visit to Duncan Spragg for information on the annular brooch. And then, on Wednesday morning, the search through the archives, in which Vince hoped to find some reference to its wearer. The brooch had become the focal point of the whole project, and Julia was determined not to think about anything else.

The next morning they were away from the Hall by ten o'clock, and to Julia's relief, Vince was brisk and businesslike. He treated her courteously, as befitted his assistant, and no more. She gave a small sigh of relief and relaxed in the car to enjoy the scenery.

It was a smooth ride on good main roads through places with romantic-sounding names like Bridge of Allan, and Auchterarder, and Broom of Dalreoch, with the fabulous mountains all around, and the legendary Allan Water bubbling and gurgling alongside. They drove through the city of Perth, with its roots embedded in the past and its claim as James the Sixth's capital of Scotland, where the River Tay produced its own riches of salmon, and pearls which were mounted by local craftsmen.

Julia begged Vince to make a short detour to see Scone, the place where the Scottish kings had been crowned, a place steeped in history and folklore. They strolled in the park at Scone Palace, where the old cross of Scone was preserved. It was no more than a fleeting visit, but to Julia it was fascinating, as was the brief glimpse of Dundee, beside the Firth of Tay, rising like a concrete jungle of buildings on the hillside above the river, with the magnificent bridge spanning the river.

Finally they turned north, up the long coastal road to Aberdeen, with the great swell of the North Sea on the right of them, and the majestic Cairngorm Mountains stretching away inland. It was a fairy-tale drive, and one that Julia wanted to imprint on her memory.

"We'll eat in a small restaurant I know outside the city," Vince remarked. "No point in battling our way through crowds of tourists and then backtracking again. You can tidy up there if you need to, and then we'll get on with our business. We needn't check into the hotel until we've seen Duncan Spragg."

It sounded sensible. Aberdeen was chockablock with tourists, and the restaurant had adequate facilities for her to wash and freshen up her makeup. Julia wore the trouser suit she'd taken to Skye, which was smart and businesslike at the same time. Her dark hair was caught back from her face with two gleaming combs of tortoiseshell, and the style emphasised her fine cheekbones and expressive violet eyes.

She was as keyed-up as Vince by the time they reached the first address, Buchanan Chambers, in a little cobbled back street in which she half expected to see Victorian gaslights and scurrying Dickensian figures. Aberdeen was a huge city, a mixture of old and new, with a university and cathedral, fine parks and a bustling harbour. Built almost entirely of granite, it was known as "the granite city," and Robert the Bruce had been one of its great benefactors.

But Mr. Buchanan turned out to be very twentieth century in appearance and approach, and reeled off vast amounts of information he'd gleaned from the letters. And by the time they left the Chambers, practically awash with very strong coffee laced with whiskey, they felt that their heads were bursting with bits of information and the monotonous drone of Mr. Buchanan's voice.

"All very interesting to him, I'm sure, but not a lot of use to us, except for clarifying some of the Gaelic terms in the documents," Vince observed. "I don't know about you, but I feel I need to clear my head. It's not far to the harbour from here. We've time for a walk, if you like."

It was just what she needed. Mr. Buchanan had been overpowering, to say the least, and the tang of the salt air was welcoming after the heavy atmosphere of his Chambers. There was a whole jumble of fishing boats jostling against each other, and also the big, seagoing ships, and a lot of foreign voices among the tourists.

"You should be here at six in the morning when the fish market opens. It's one of the biggest in Britain, and very popular with tourists, for some reason. Still, it gets them on to an early start to see the city," Vince told her.

She nodded. She was watching the progress of a dozen or so Americans, armed with cameras and maps, wearing an amazing assortment of plaid jackets and trousers. She turned to comment on them to Vince, but he was looking at his watch and telling her they'd better start looking for Duncan Spragg's establishment if they were going to get there by four o'clock.

They found it quite easily. It was little more than an unobtrusive brown door in a busy street when seen from the outside, but inside there was a receptionist's office, and then Mr. Spragg's office, a brown-panelled room with a large window, in front of which was a desk covered with papers and files, a pair of metal weighing scales, jewellers' eyeglasses and so on.

Duncan Spragg was a small man in a brown suit. He might have been anything from fifty to seventy, with wispy grey-brown hair. The overall effect of the room was brown, Julia thought. But his smile was welcoming and he asked them to sit down and pulled a file marked Galbraith toward him. As he opened it, Julia saw a sheet of paper headed Assay Report. She felt a tingle of anticipation.

"Well now, Mr. Galbraith, I have some very good news for you. The brooch is a very fine piece indeed. In an absolutely shocking state when it came to me, of course, but I think you'll agree that it's vastly improved now."

He reached into a drawer beside him and drew out a small box. He removed the lid almost reverently, and placed it on the desk in front of them. Julia caught her breath in a gasp.

The annular brooch lay on a bed of cream-coloured silk, showing it to best advantage. It had been cleaned and polished to a gleaming perfection, the leaves and interlacing exquisitely defined in the heavy silver. In its centre, like a glowing spider caught in a silver web, was the emerald, richly breathtaking.

Even Vince seemed too stunned to speak for a few minutes.

"You've done a remarkable job, Mr. Spragg," he said at last, his voice husky. "I do congratulate you on the transformation."

The small man smiled slightly. "It's not difficult to beautify something that is already perfect," he said. "The brooch could not have been worn in battle very often, if at all. Usually such pieces are sadly marked by weapons, and the jewel dislodged. But the silver is almost unmarked, and the emerald intact. We have been very fortunate."

He beamed at them both as if he was in part possession. But Julia could completely understand his joy in exposing the beauty of the brooch. He reminded her in many ways of Mr. Pollard, her ex-boss. She was impatient to know more, as was Vince. He motioned toward the Assay Report and the file.

"Ah, yes." Mr. Spragg put a pair of half-moon glasses on to peer down at the papers. He knew how to keep them in suspense, Julia thought, with a glance at Vince. "I'd place the brooch at about four hundred years old, Mr. Galbraith, and most likely it was used solely as a betrothal piece, because of the lack of battle scars on it, as I've said. Value . . ." He drew in his breath in a small whistle. "Upwards of six thousand pounds."

There was a stunned silence in the room for a few minutes, and then Duncan Spragg removed his glasses, stood up and came around the desk to shake Vince by the hand vigourously.

"If I may make a suggestion, Mr. Galbraith, a museum would be very honoured to display it for you, and it would be in safekeeping. . . ."

"Thank you, Mr. Spragg. If I need any advice on that I shall certainly be in touch with you," Vince assured him. "Perhaps I can leave it here tonight and collect it tomorrow morning on our way to the archives? Say about nine-thirty?"

"Of course. It will be quite safe locked up here." He made to close the box, but Vince stopped him with a smile. He picked the brooch out of its silky nest and held it in his hand for a moment, running his finger over the delicate filigree work before handing it to Julia to hold.

It was quite heavy, though it was barely three inches in diameter. Julia had held many valuable objects in her hands during the course of her work, but none quite so sensational as this. And the feeling came as much from the journey she and Vince had made to find it as from the value of the brooch itself. Not to mention the thought of the craftsman who had made it all those years ago. . . .

"How does it feel to be holding six thousand pounds' worth of brooch in your hand?" Vince's voice came to her ears.

"Beyond explaining." She handed it back with a little shake of her head, more moved by the piece than she had expected.

There was still the copper brooch to be dealt with, of course, but Duncan Spragg identified that one easily, and with no need to refer to other sources. The small man shook hands with them and showed them out; clearly, they were important clients. The annular brooch had been safely locked away in their presence, and they came out into the late afternoon sunlight feeling slightly bowled over.

"It seems inadequate to suggest a cup of tea," Julia murmured. "But my throat is so dry I need one."

"So do I," Vince tucked her hand in his arm and strode off in the direction of some old-fashioned tearooms along the street. "But later it's going to be champagne for you and me, my sweet. It's not every day something like this happens!"

He was in an exuberant mood, and she could hardly blame him. He was at his most charming . . . his most dangerous, as far as she was concerned, and she reminded herself not to let it all go to her head. But she could hardly help feeling elated, too. She had been part of his search, after all, and they had never expected to come across anything like this. It was a spectacular bonus.

"I wonder just how it came to be in Old Hamish's possession," Julia commented when the waitress had put the pot of tea and a selection of cream cakes in front of them.

"We'll probably never know for certain. As far as he's concerned, it was 'Graindfaither's box,' and that's the end of it. It's most certainly a Galbraith piece, though. Maybe one of his ancestors was given it for services rendered. Maybe one of them stole it." Vince shrugged. It would probably remain a mystery forever, and maybe it was better so.

These were the best times, Julia thought suddenly. When they were both so intent on the job they'd set out to do, and there were no emotional hang-ups on either side. They were a team. If only it could stay that way she could get through the next couple of days. . . .

They reached the hotel around six o'clock. The car park was almost full, and there were several busses parked there as well. It was a very large hotel,

almost castlelike with its spires and turrets. Several
flags were flying outside, and when they entered the
foyer the first thing they saw was a banner across the
entrance saying "Welcome to our American
Friends." The whole place seemed to be swarming
with similar plaid-garbed smiling figures such as
they'd seen near the fish market.

"I forgot to mention—there's an American Convention going on here this week," Vince said into
her ear above the din. "You know the kind of
thing—looking up their roots. More or less what
we're doing, I suppose, except they're a bit noisier
when there's a crowd of them!"

She looked at him with sudden suspicion. It didn't
really matter, of course, and maybe it was better to
have a crowd of people around, but why hadn't he
bothered to tell her?

"Look, there are a couple of seats in the lounge
over there. Go and grab them, Julia, while I fight my
way through to the desk and get our keys. I'll have a
couple of sherries sent over."

"Oh, but . . ." She didn't particularly want any
sherry, but he'd already disappeared among the
crowd of Americans with their overnight cases. She
gave a shrug and found the two seats, and within
minutes a waiter had put two glasses of sherry in
front of her. She was jostled on all sides by the jovial
Americans, who were eventually rounded up by
their courier to change for dinner.

"Phew! I was beginning to feel like a specimen."
She grinned.

"It's that lovely Cornish cream accent of yours."
He smiled back. "They're just beginning to get used
to the Scots one by now, and yours is a novelty.
Anyway, we'd better get changed, too. You've time
for a shower before dinner if you like. There's a
bathroom attached to the room. Number 143."

He handed her an ornate key and said he'd see her
later, and that the cases had already been taken

upstairs. There was a lift just across the foyer. She was glad to get away from the crowd—and from Vince—and to be on her own for a little while. She found the room at the end of a long corridor and unlocked the door with a sigh of relief.

The first thing she noticed was the double bed. And then the two overnight cases side by side on the slatted stool. She stared at them for a few seconds. They'd made a mistake, she thought immediately. She picked up the house phone. It was answered a little impatiently, and she could hear the buzz of noise in the background.

"I'm sorry, but could you let Mr. Galbraith know his case is in room 143, please? I think there's been a mistake with the cases."

"No mistake, Mrs. Galbraith. Room 143. I'm sorry, but if you've any complaints, I did explain that it was the only room available, what with the convention this week. Mr. Galbraith understood that when he booked it."

"I see. Thank you," she said quickly, as his voice became more affronted. She banged the phone down, aware of a slow fury taking hold of her. *Mrs. Galbraith*, the man had said.

So this was what it had all been about . . . the secrecy, the apparent disregard of her phone calls with Andrew, the little quiet lunch at the restaurant so that they didn't get here until it was too late to do anything about it . . . the double room, all ready for the big seduction scene. . . .

The click of the door sounded behind her, and she whirled round to see Vince standing there, a second key in his hand.

"How dare you do this to me?" she said in a choked voice. "Did you really think I'd stay here with you like this?"

"You have no other choice. The hotel's absolutely full, and every other place in the city is the same."

"I do have a choice! I'll take a train or a bus back

to Glasgow and go to Aunt Meg's," she said furiously. "You can't keep me here against my will. . . ."

He was across the room with a few long strides, his arms closing round her in an iron-hard embrace. "Do you think I want you against your will? But you're so stubborn it was the only way I could think of to have some time alone with you when you couldn't escape me. What is it you're so afraid of, Julia? That you'll let me see through that icy exterior to just how much of a woman you are?"

"Let me go." She struggled against him, but he was unrelenting.

"Are you so afraid to be alone with me?" His voice softened.

"No . . . I just don't like your way of going about things, that's all. Passing me off as your *wife*, for instance. I don't like being put into an impossible position like this. I don't want to share a room with you. . . ." She was aware that there was a sudden panic in her voice, and that he knew it. No doubt Isla wouldn't have had any such reservations, she thought bitterly. What about the weekend she and Vince had spent together last summer? Had she been "Mrs. Galbraith" then?

He suddenly held her more tenderly. A change of tactics . . . She tried to keep the anger intact, but it was difficult when his lips suddenly brushed her cheek and the fresh tang of his aftershave was sharp in her nostrils.

"Will you believe me when I tell you that this hotel really was fully booked when I rang them?" he asked softly. "And that I had to twist somebody's arm to give us a room at all?"

"But not two rooms?" she couldn't help saying bitterly.

Vince gave her a little shake. "No, not two rooms. But if it'll make you feel better, we can always put a pillow in the bed between us."

He was laughing at her now.

"I've no intention of sleeping in the same bed as you. You can have the armchair. . . ."

"I've no intention of sleeping in a chair all night with a long drive in front of me tomorrow, and we'll have no such nonsense." Vince's mood was changing swiftly. "I promise you'll be quite safe from my advances unless you make it obvious . . . ?"

Julia felt her face go hot. "Will you please let go of me so that I can have my bath now?" she asked stiffly. "I suppose you'll allow me *some* privacy?"

He released her at once, and she picked up her case and marched to the adjoining bathroom, slamming the bolt behind her. She was shaking all over. Nothing could have prepared her for this, and she wished the next twelve hours were over. She heard him call out to her not to be all night in there, and she jumped as if she'd been stung, hurrying through her routine, overconscious of his movements in the bedroom on the other side of the door.

She'd brought the turquoise dress for the evening, and slipped it over her head with a gesture of defiance, dotting her throat and pulse-points with perfume. It was all for nothing as far as Vince Galbraith was concerned, she thought savagely, for she was certainly not making it obvious that she wanted any attentions from him. . . .

His eyes wandered slowly over her when she emerged from the bathroom. She had highlighted her eyes and cheekbones, and let her hair hang loosely about her shoulders. Her skin glowed, and she heard his small intake of breath as he watched her move across the room and slip her feet into high-heeled sandals.

"Hadn't you better get ready?" There was a small catch in her voice, because she really didn't want him looking at her like that. The situation was too intimate, and though she knew she was subtly taunting him, she had to keep things cool between them or she was lost. He turned abruptly and went into the bathroom.

Twenty minutes later he was back, in a dark suit and silk shirt and tie. He looked devastating, as always, and she caught sight of them both in the mirror. On the surface, they looked what they were supposed to be . . . a very attractive young couple. Julia moved quickly to her jewel box and opened it with shaking hands. This was something she had to do, that had been in her mind ever since Vince had sprung this impossible situation on her.

"Do you remember me telling you once that I was involved with someone else?" Her voice was suddenly muffled, and she could feel the tension between them. She drew out Martin's engagement ring, which she always kept with her, and pulled it slowly onto her finger, turning toward him as she did so. She held out her hand, aware that it wouldn't quite stop trembling. "What I didn't tell you was that I was engaged, Vince."

His look said he didn't believe her, and she rushed on.

"His name is Martin Tregorran, and he's the reason I can't be—what you expect." She didn't quite know how to put it delicately.

He crossed toward her, not touching her, his eyes almost boring into hers. "If this is true, then what are you doing here?" he asked harshly. "And what kind of man lets a girl like you get away from him, with never a letter or a phone call? Do you take me for an idiot, Julia?"

She looked at him numbly. It had been her trump card, but she hadn't stopped to think that he'd be shrewd enough to see through it in a minute.

"Take it from me that I love Martin very much." Her voice was vibrant with conviction. "And that I've no intention of betraying him with you or anybody else."

She pushed past him and opened the door. He reached her before she got to the lift and they rode down in silence. In the dining room, they were obliged to share a table with four of the Americans, who kept up a lively conversation the whole time, drawing them into it against their will. It was a relief to Julia. She let them flirt harmlessly with her, seeing the sparkle of anger in Vince's eyes and caring nothing for it. True to his word, he bought them champagne, and included the Americans in the gesture. It wasn't going to be quite the celebration he had imagined for the two of them.

She spun out the evening as long as she could, accepting for both of them the Americans' invitation to join them in the lounge bar. Vince glowered along beside her, but finally even the Americans called it a day, and he put a casual arm around her shoulders in front of them all, knowing she couldn't object. His lips nuzzled into her neck, bringing guffaws of laughter from the rest of the little group.

"Time we went to bed, isn't it, sweetheart?" he said seductively. "We've got to be up early in the morning."

She kept the smile fixed on her face as he went on teasing her, but once inside their room she blazed at him. "I suppose you thought that was clever?" she snapped. He caught hold of her wrist in an iron grip.

"Oh, I can be as clever as you—and since you were giving such a good impression of the loving little wife, I thought I'd add to the illusion."

"Well, you can forget it now." She wrenched away from him.

"Naturally." His voice was cold as he turned back the bedcovers and elaborately placed a pillow down the centre of the bed. "Can I trust you not to molest me in the middle of the night? You can use the bathroom first, then I'll give you ten minutes to hide beneath the bedclothes, if that's what you intend doing!"

165

Julia glared at him. "I'm not likely to faint away at the sight of a man's pajamas like some Victorian maiden."

Vince grinned. "Who said anything about pajamas?"

Julia's face flamed. All right, so she was pretending to be totally modern and permissive, but she might have known she couldn't go through with it. It just wasn't her style.

"If that was supposed to be funny—"

"I don't think it's in the least funny." He was enjoying her embarrassment. His eyes followed the taut lines of her shape in a lazy, insolent gaze. "In fact, I'm quite serious about all this."

Julia swallowed, her throat suddenly dry. "Vince, I'm asking you not to do this." She spoke with a catch in her breath, her voice thick. "All right. I accept the fact that we do have to share this room for the night, but can't you see that you'll make it impossible for us to go on working together if you—if you—"

He caught her in his arms. "If I what, sweetheart?" His voice was seductively low. "If I do what we both want so much? Just how long are you going to go on denying it?"

Julia closed her eyes for a moment so that she didn't have to look into the penetrating dark gaze, or at the sensuous, demanding mouth. But she couldn't be indifferent to the way his hands were moving caressingly up and down her back, circling the curves of her hips, moulding her to him. . . .

"I don't deny it." The words trembled on her lips, forcing themselves to be said. "But I have no intention of being unfaithful to Martin. I've never betrayed him, and whatever your standards are, they're not mine."

Her voice gained strength as she felt Vince's hands stop their seductive movements. She'd brought Martin's name between them deliberately. It seemed to be having the effect she'd wanted, though she knew full well she was yet again denying herself the chance of happiness in Vince's arms. But not like this . . . not because of his clever little scheme. She hoped the little barb that he was quite happy to be two-timing Isla had stirred his conscience a bit, too. Because she didn't know how much longer she could hold out against him if it hadn't. . . .

As she felt his arms let her go, Julia jerked away from him and sped toward the bathroom, snatching up her case as she went. Inside, she leaned against the door for a moment, trying to stop the frantic thumping of her heart. Her hands were still shaking as she cleaned her teeth and removed her makeup, then, after a minute's hesitation, she changed into her nightdress and the Chinese robe. She'd felt tempted to stay fully clothed all night, but she didn't want to wake up all creased and uncomfortable, and maybe now she'd made her feelings so plain that Vince would realise she meant what she said.

She went back to the bedroom as coolly as she could, and Vince passed her without a word to go into the bathroom himself. She slid out of the robe and dived into the bed, feeling quite ridiculous as she felt the lengthways pillow down its middle, but she made no attempt to remove it.

She wished desperately that she'd brought a different nightdress with her, and not the diaphanous one she was wearing. Not that Vince was going to get a glimpse of it . . . if she could help it.

"Is it safe to come in?" His voice came suddenly from the foot of the bed. "You don't have this elusive Martin at the end of the telephone to keep us company all night, do you?"

Julia's heart lurched. Vince could have no idea how his words wounded her, of course, and she began to wish she'd never started this charade. "Don't be ridiculous," she said unsteadily.

She saw him stride toward the bed before she

closed her eyes quickly. But she couldn't blot out the image of him, in black silk pajama trousers and nothing else. His shoulders were broad and muscled, his chest matted with dark hair that tapered to his waist. His skin was smooth and bronzed; he hadn't an ounce of spare flesh on him. She felt the bed give beneath his weight as he lay on the other side of it, the extra pillow between them. . . .

It was impossible to sleep. Julia was far too aware of him, and of the fact that he wasn't sleeping either. Once, she threw out her arm in a relaxed manner, to draw it back at once as her fingers touched his face.

"You don't have to slap me before I've done anything," Vince's voice came out of the darkness. "Or was that just in anticipation?"

"Of course not. I'm sorry." She knew she sounded stilted, but she dared not relax her guard.

"Did you know that courting couples behave like this in some parts of the world?" he said next, his voice very controlled. "Their families allow them to sleep together with a pillow or plank between them in the fond belief it will keep them apart. Can you really imagine any couple who were madly in love letting anything so futile keep them apart?"

Julia's heart was beating very unevenly. No, she couldn't imagine it. It was more than flesh and blood could bear. . . . Suddenly she realised that Vince had tossed the dividing pillow out of the bed. She could see his dark shape in the light from the window as he leaned over her, and the next second she was enveloped in his arms.

"Vince, you promised—" She could hardly breathe as one of his hands reached for her breast, hidden under the diaphanous nightdress. She might as well have been naked for all the good it did anyway. . . .

"I don't remember promising anything, except to myself," he said thickly. "You and I have played cat and mouse for long enough, my lovely Julia."

The lean length of his body covered hers. His mouth was demanding on her own, and every part of her sought the fulfillment he offered. But not like this . . . not thrust on her because of circumstances, whether he had deliberately engineered them or not. His thighs were pressing tightly down on hers, moving sensuously and slowly. She felt as if she would slowly melt into the softness of the bed at his insistent, relentless seduction.

"I'll never forgive you if you go on with this." Her voice trembled and her lips were sore where she had bitten them. But she would not give in willingly. He would have to take her by force if he took her at all. She would not help him; it was a matter of pride now. She would not let him have his full triumph, not let him know how much she yearned for the sweetness of his loving, only to have him reject her for Isla tomorrow. . . .

Julia clenched her hands at her sides, forcing herself to remain perfectly still in his embrace. Never by a flicker would she let him know how she was affected by him, nor what exquisite sensations were shooting through her. It took a few mintues for him to realise what she was doing, that she was not responding to his caresses except by the shortening of her breath. But slowly Julia became aware that his passion was lessening, until finally he swore abruptly and rolled away from her. She could hardly believe it. She had won . . . but nothing had ever seemed less like a victory. Minutes later, she heard him pulling on his clothes again in the darkness.

"I know a little club near here that stays open all night," Vince said harshly. "I'll take myself off there for an hour or so, since my company is obviously so repugnant to you. Get to sleep, and I'll try not to waken you when I get back. And I hope your dreams of Martin will console you."

The next minute he was gone, and Julia lay alone in the bed in stunned silence. She was so tense with the effort of trying not to move when everything in her had been crying out to respond to him that she ached all over. Suddenly she seemed to crumple in the bed and wept into the pillow. What the blazes was the matter with her? She loved him wildly, even though he infuriated and enraged her. She loved him more than she'd ever thought it possible to love a man, and she was the one who was putting up all the barriers between them. Because of Isla, a cold little voice inside reminded her. Because he'd never said he loved her, and without love the rest meant nothing. . . .

Or so she'd always thought, until now. But now he'd gone and there was just this unfulfilled ache inside her. Was she so clever after all, when she could have snatched this one night's happiness with him? Would one night have mattered so much to Isla, if he was truly going to marry her?

Her head throbbed. She didn't even know that for sure. She'd simply taken Fern's word for it. She'd probably messed up everything between her and Vince because of a child's spite. Her fingers touched the coldness of her engagement ring as she clenched her hands together. And she'd added to the distance between them, she thought bitterly, by pretending that Martin was still alive.

Eventually she drifted off to sleep from sheer exhaustion, and she didn't hear Vince come back. She was dreaming . . . in a beautiful world where time and space ceased to matter anymore, and there were only two people in it. There was a sand-covered beach and a boat waiting to drift silently out to the middle of a glassy ocean, and two people stepping aboard . . . herself in a diaphanous white gown through which her body was clearly visible . . . and Vince, darkly handsome in a pair of light-coloured trousers and bare feet, his magnificent chest rippling as he pushed the boat into the water, the dark hairs catching the sunlight in their hazel flecks. Just like his eyes . . . she was getting terribly muddled in the dream as his arms were held out to her and she melted into them gladly . . . wantonly. . . .

She was suddenly wide awake and it was daylight. The arms that were holding her were real, and the warmth of Vince's body caressed hers as his lips sought her mouth. She was unable to resist his kiss.

"I wish I could wake up this way every single morning." He spoke almost angrily. "With you in my arms and that beautifully vulnerable look in your eyes. That half-sleeping look that sees no one but me!"

She pushed him away from her then, her heart pounding as the memory of her dream rushed back to her. Last night . . . before he had gone storming out of the hotel . . . and then her dream . . . if it *had* all been a dream. . . .

"Vince," she whispered. "You, you didn't—"

He swung his legs out of the bed and padded across to the bathroom. He walked insolently, with the walk of a sleek black cat in his black silk pajama trousers, and her mouth was suddenly dry. At the last moment, he turned to look at her as she lay with her hair a tangled cloud on the pillow.

"No, my darling," he mocked her. "Much as I love you, not even *I* could take advantage of you while you slept, but if you don't get out of that bed and get dressed pretty soon I might start having second thoughts about my gentlemanly habits. I know you don't think too much of them as it is."

Chapter Ten

Julia stared numbly out the hotel window. The Americans were already piling into their busses after an early breakfast.

Much as I love you, Vince had said. . . .

She waved as one of the group from last night caught sight of her at the window.

Much as I love you, he'd said. . . . She couldn't get the words out of her head. Such talk was cheap, Julia told herself shakily. He hadn't meant it . . . and yet, if he'd wanted her that much, surely the time for glib talk had been last night. If he had but realised it, all he'd needed to do was be convincing enough in saying that he loved her. Even if it hadn't been true . . . But he hadn't said it last night. He'd said it now, when it was too late for anything— but the truth.

He came out of the bathroom, telling her it was all hers and to get moving. He was his usual brisk self, and she moved into action, telling herself his words really hadn't meant a thing, and she wasn't going to start mooning over them now, when this trip to the archives this morning was going to be one of their last together.

She told him so over breakfast.

"You can't leave me now, with the job half done."
He stared at her, the dark eyes brooding again.

"You don't need me, Vince. You never really did,
did you? If you'd never met me, the book would still
have got finished. . . ."

"Of course I need you! Haven't I been telling you
that ever since I met you?" His tone was aggressive,
and she glanced toward some interested fellow
guests.

"I've made up my mind. At the end of the week,
I'm going back to Aunt Meg's, and then," she kept
her eyes on her plate, "I may go back to Cornwall.
My job there is always open to me."

"Back to this Martin whatever his name is, who
can't even be bothered to keep in touch with you, I
suppose?"

She looked up then. He was obviously holding his
temper in check with an effort, and she could see he
considered her a fool if what he believed was true.

"That's right. Back to Martin," she said evenly.
"And I really don't want to discuss my private life
with you any longer. Did you arrange any special
time to be at the archives?"

He didn't answer for a minute, and she felt the
colour run up her cheeks. She felt as if he could see
right through her, but then he shrugged.

"As soon as we like, so we may as well check out
when we've finished. And by the way—you've forgotten your engagement ring again. This Martin of
yours doesn't seem to inspire you with much romantic feeling, does he? I wonder if Andrew Macleod
knows about him."

Julia bit her lips. All she wanted was to get out of
here, to work until the end of the week and then out
of his life. The very thought of it gave her a bleak,
empty feeling, but she couldn't go on living like this,
loving Vince and being so tormented by him.

"Why don't you tell him—and Isla, too? Tell

everybody!" she said wildly. She got to her feet and told him she'd wait for him in the foyer while he handed in their keys. She couldn't face one more hotel clerk calling her Mrs. Galbraith. . . .

They drove to the archives in silence. Julia tried to recapture the delight from their meeting with Duncan Spragg yesterday, but it had evaporated overnight. While she started going through some old pictorial records, Vince went back to Spragg's establishment to fetch the annular brooch. She was deep into her research when he returned.

"I think I've found something," she told him. She handed him the photostats of the original documents, stored safely in the vaults. But there were definitely crude drawings of the annular brooch, pinned high on the plaid of a highlander ready for battle, one of Vince's ancestors and a detailed account of the occasion on which it was worn on the betrothal of one Lydia Monroe to Alistair Galbraith. It had no doubt been Lydia who had kept the brooch as a keepsake and a love token after the betrothal. . . .

"That's great stuff," he said enthusiastically. "Just the kind of thing I was hoping to find. Now we'll just go through this other list if you can take some notes, Julia."

They worked steadily until noon, when Vince decided that they had had enough. Julia stretched. Her shoulder blades ached, and he suddenly got up and stood behind her, kneading them gently until the pain went out of them. It was as well she couldn't see the expression on his face at that moment, but she was very aware of his caressing fingers.

"Better?" he asked roughly.

She nodded. "Let's get out of here, Vince. I've had enough of old things for now. I feel the need to get the wind in my hair and the sun on my face."

"Come on, then. Next stop the open hills, and we'll breathe in some good fresh air."

They drove out of Aberdeen, stopping at the same little restaurant as yesterday for lunch, and then drove back along the coast. It was a strangely poignant journey for Julia, knowing they were soon to part. She could take little interest in the scenery this time. But once through Perth, Vince took a different road, climbing through narrow dirt roads into the hills, where pretty little glens nestled between towering crags, and burns chattered and sang, their crystal-clear waters dancing in the sunlight. He stopped the car on a grassy spot overlooking a small still loch, and they both got out and stretched their legs. It was so quiet they might have been in another world, and Julia drank in great lungfuls of the pure air.

"It's beautiful," she breathed.

"Yes, it is," he told her, and she knew he wasn't referring just to the scenery. He made no attempt to touch her, and she was both relieved and disappointed. But she'd brought all this on herself, and she knew it.

"I think it's as well that you're leaving," he said suddenly. Her heart jolted at his words.

"You do?" she stammered.

"I couldn't go on seeing you every day of my life without wanting to make love to you," he told her baldly. "It's driving me out of my mind."

"I'm—sorry." She didn't know if it was the right reply to make. He looked at her thoughtfully.

"Are you? Then give me one last kiss to remember you by. One kiss as if you meant it, while there's no one in the world to know about it but the two of us. No Martin—"

"Or Isla?"

"Or Isla." He shrugged. He held out his arms to her, and Julia went into them as if this was still part of her dream, melting against him as if she was part of him, feeling every fibre of him shape itself to her body as if they were the same person. Her arms wound round his neck as his mouth sought hers and took it in an enchanted embrace from which she never wanted to escape. . . .

And then Vince was unwinding her arms from his neck and putting her deliberately away from him. She was breathing very fast, all her senses alive, her body craving for more. . . .

"And you remember *that* the next time your Martin takes you in his arms," he said cruelly.

"Vince—" The lump in her throat was choking her. She had to swallow hard. But he wasn't listening to her. He was already walking to the car, and he might have been a million miles away where only seconds ago they'd been so close in mind and body.

"We'll get back now." He was coldly distant, as if he had achieved his purpose and wanted nothing more to do with her. Julia's legs felt wobbly as she walked slowly toward the car and sat beside him. He slammed his door and looked straight ahead. "And if you're determined to leave at the end of the week, perhaps we should concoct some story that I don't need you for a while, but leave it open. It will only cause a fuss between Rose and Meggie if they think there's some upset between us. All right?"

Julia nodded. She hadn't considered her aunt at all. She'd just thought of Strathrowan as a refuge, the way she had after Martin died. But Vince had a point, of course. It would be embarrassing for Aunt Meg if she guessed that she and Vince were so antagonistic toward each other . . . but "some upset," as he put it, was the understatement of the year!

He drove off in the direction of Glasgow now, leaving the quiet glens and the mountains as soon as they reached the main roads, and the magic that had flared so ecstatically between them might never have been. Vince concentrated grimly on his driving, and she couldn't think of anything to say until they were nearing the last climb to Galbraith Hall.

"Vince, I should have told you about Martin . . ." she began slowly. Unconsciously, she circled her bare engagement finger with her right hand.

"Yes, you should have." His voice was harsh. "Whatever you think of me, Julia, I'm not in the habit of taking something that belongs to another man. Why you don't wear your engagement ring is your own business, but if you were mine I'd make sure there wasn't any doubt, nor would I let you go gallivanting round the country making sheeps' eyes at poor fools like Andrew Macleod!"

She gasped angrily. "Well, I'm not yours, nor ever likely to be," she snapped. "And if that's the way you'd treat your wife, as some kind of chattel, then Isla Macleod is very welcome to you, thank you very much!"

"What has Isla got to do with it?"

"Everything, I should have thought! Ask Fern! Anyway, I don't want to discuss my private life, nor yours. And the sooner I can arrange to leave Galbraith Hall, the better. But I promise I'll be discreet about my reasons. I'd hate to spoil your virile image by letting anyone think a woman actually turned you down!" She was as sarcastic as she could be, the words tumbling out as he yanked the brake on outside the Hall. She didn't wait for any reply, opened the door and stalked inside, leaving him to bring the small cases.

Rose was out, and Julia breathed a sigh of relief, then went straight to the phone and was dialling her aunt's number by the time Vince had garaged the car and came into the house.

"Yes, Aunt Meg, I had a lovely time, but we did go there on business, you know!" She tried to make her voice light. "Anyway, I'm ringing to say Vince doesn't need me for a few weeks now, so I'd like to come and stay at Strathrowan again if you'll have me. I need to unwind after the hectic life of the past few weeks!"

"Of course you can come," Julia heard her aunt say, and relief flooded through her. "Shall I fetch you?"

Vince was hovering in the hall, his face dark and tight. He couldn't have heard her aunt's words, but he suddenly said he'd be going into Glasgow on Friday afternoon and he'd drop her off then. Julia relayed the message woodenly. It was what she wanted—what she felt she had to do, but it was suddenly all so final. The end of another episode in her life, and she had to start picking up the pieces all over again. And between then and Friday she seemed to be living in a kind of limbo.

Vince had told Rose he'd got as far as he could with his project for the time being and would be concentrating on the estate business for a few weeks and then maybe Julia would come back again for some polishing up of the rough draft of his book. Thankfully, she believed him.

"I'm glad you're not going for good, Julia," Rose told her with a cool smile. "You've been good for Vince, apart from helping him."

She let Rose go on thinking the arrangement was only temporary, and anyway, Rose was too overwhelmed by the enormity of the finds from Hamish Buckie's cottage to probe too deeply. Vince had told her he would make more provisions for the old man, and she was touched by his concern. He had no need to do anything, really, because everything in the tin box had been Galbraith property, but Vince would feel it his moral duty to see that Old Hamish didn't go unrewarded. He had his good points, Julia conceded.

But it was something of a relief when Friday came and she was leaving the Hall behind her. She barely glanced at the mirrored surface of Loch Lomond as it came into view round bend after bend in the road. She was too tense to do anything but stare straight ahead and wish this last journey over. She had some vague idea of leaving Scotland for good in a week or so, but that was something she was keeping to herself for the time being. No need to start Aunt Meg wondering. . . .

If Vince had wanted a few private moments with her before he let her out of the car, he was doomed to disappointment, because her aunt was in the garden, taking off the heads of the last of the summer roses. Neither of them had been very talkative, Julia thought miserably, and when Aunt Meg asked him in for some tea he shook his head at once.

"Not today, Meggie, thanks. I'm going to see Isla and we're off dancing tonight."

Thanks, for telling me, Julia thought. It was the last little twist of the knife. He unloaded her cases and took them in, and then he was gone. As far as Aunt Meg knew, the job was still on, of course, and this was just a temporary good-bye.

Julia's eyes were damp as she took the cases to her old room. It was good-bye forever, she thought. Good-bye, my love, my once-in-a-lifetime love. . . . Maybe she was one of those women destined never to find fulfillment, she thought with a burst of self-pity. First Martin . . . now Vince. . . .

"Well, you look as though he's been working you pretty hard," Aunt Meg remarked when she went downstairs for a welcome cup of tea.

"It's been very interesting, though," Julia said. At least that was true. Vince didn't want any news of the annular brooch to leak out until he'd got it properly insured, but she was free to tell Aunt Meg about the copper one, and the two days in Aberdeen, and the Americans.

"They're so enthusiastic." Julia grinned. "They were intrigued by my accent, too, after so many Scots ones. It was certainly an eventful couple of days."

You could say that again, she told herself. And

finding herself in Vince's arms in bed on Wednesday morning hadn't exactly been the most unpleasant part of it, either. . . . Her hands shook a little as she drank her tea. She gave a deep sigh.

"But tiring?" Aunt Meg looked at her keenly.

"Oh, yes! All I want to do is sleep round the clock tonight, and then walk myself back to normal for the next few days."

"Sounds a bit like back to square one," her aunt commented. "You said something very much like that when you first came here. But things are better now, aren't they, love? I mean, about Martin . . ."

"Yes." Julia gave a crooked little smile. "I suppose I've discovered that nothing lasts forever, not even grief, Aunt Meg. It's a sobering thought, isn't it?"

She was in a state she could compare to suspended animation, Julia thought. She'd been back in Strathrowan for a week, and in some ways it had been the longest week of her life. Even the week after Martin died had been filled with activity, and with people . . . so many things to do and arrange . . . but this week had been nothing like that. Aunt Meg had her own friends and her own way of life, and all their sightseeing had already been done.

Besides, Julia had assured her that all she wanted was time to herself, to walk the hills and enjoy the freedom and the glorious autumn while it lasted. It had been a long warm summer, and the fine weather was holding on longer than usual. When it ended, there would be little chance to enjoy the hills as she could now.

But instead of having their healing powers, this time the solitude of the hills and the whispering bracken kept reminding her of Vince. She kept seeing his face in all its moods; she heard his voice in the sigh of the wind; she felt the touch of his lips on hers as the sunshine warmed them. She dreamed of him, waking and sleeping. She was lost . . . loving him so much it was sweet torment to be still here in his little corner of the world.

She began to feel panicky. As if she was stateless, adrift in a sea of loneliness from which there was no escape. For how could she escape her own feelings?

He could have phoned her, just once, she thought resentfully. Even if he didn't want to ask her out, he might have phoned. Or was he so busy with Isla that he never gave her a second thought now? She had given him the impression that she was still engaged to Martin, so she had no one to blame but herself for being left strictly alone.

"You fool," she whispered to herself through a mist of tears one Sunday morning, the second Sunday since coming back to her aunt's cottage. "You blind, crazy fool, throwing away your second chance of happiness."

Her tear-blurred eyes caught the vivid yellow of the gorse bushes on her way down to the cottage. The flowers that Martin used to tease her about . . . "when the gorse is in bloom, it's the kissing time . . ." Martin would never have begrudged her this second chance, but she'd been the one to throw it all away. . . . Even the faces of the blossom seemed to reproach her.

By the time she got back to the cottage for Sunday lunch, a delicious smell of roast beef met her nose. But she hardly ate a thing, pushing the food round her plate and protesting that she just wasn't very hungry.

"Well, you should be," Aunt Meg said shortly. "A walk on the hills is supposed to give you an appetite, but it doesn't seem to be doing you a lot of good lately. Why don't you come over to see Rose with me this afternoon? I'm going over for tea, and I think she's a bit fed up because Vince has been like a bear with a sore head all the week."

"I'd rather not, if you don't mind, Aunt Meg," she murmured. "I've got a slight headache."

Her aunt muttered something that Julia didn't catch, and she tried to make amends by saying she'd wash the dishes if Aunt Meg wanted to leave them for her. At least it gave her something to do for half an hour, though the cottage felt very lonely after her aunt had gone off in the chugging old Ford.

She tried reading some magazines, but the words danced in front of her and she couldn't concentrate. The walking had made her tired, and she must have dozed off in one of the comfortable armchairs, because suddenly she heard a car door slamming and awoke with a start. It was only four-thirty, she saw with a glance at the clock. Why had Aunt Meg come back . . . ?

The door suddenly opened, and Vince's large figure was blocking out the light. Julia felt her heart start to pound as she jumped up too quickly, and her head swam dizzily. What did he want? She couldn't cope with another scene with him.

He was across the tiny room in two strides, kicking the door shut behind him and pulling her into his arms.

"Why didn't you tell me?" he demanded roughly.

"Tell you what?" Her voice was faint.

"The truth about Martin. Why did you let me think you were still engaged to him, when he had that terrible accident three weeks before your wedding? My poor, sweet darling, why didn't you tell me?"

This couldn't be happening, Julia thought. It was still part of her dream . . . the dream where he held her close and his eyes were tender, and all the anger between them had gone. . . .

"Aunt Meg," she said weakly. "She promised not to say anything. I didn't want anyone's pity. . . ."

"Thank God I caught her in an unguarded moment this afternoon, then. Rose and I were having a bit of a battle when she arrived for tea today, and I suppose I was sounding off a little, and poor old Meggie unwittingly added to it by saying you hadn't been in very good spirits since you went back to Strathrowan either." He suddenly stroked Julia's dark hair back from her forehead, seeing the smudgy shadows under her eyes—eyes that seemed even deeper in colour in the pallour of her skin.

"I'm afraid I turned on Meggie at that moment, and nearly snapped her head off, sweetheart. I told her it was a pity you didn't get back to Cornwall where you belonged and put this Martin out of his misery then. She realised I knew something about Martin, but not all of it, and she blurted it all out in a fury. It was like being hit between the eyes with a sledgehammer."

She couldn't say anything. The lump in her throat was too thick.

"Poor old Meggie," he went on ruefully. "She was upset because she'd betrayed your confidence, but I told her I'd put it right with you. You aren't going to blame her, are you, Julia?"

He tipped up her chin to look deep in her eyes, and she shook her head wordlessly. It was a tremendous relief that he knew after all, even though she wasn't sure where that left the two of them. . . .

"You must have thought I was a brute, acting the way I did," he said softly. "If I'd known the truth, I might have gone more slowly. As it was . . . I suppose it was a bit of a shock to my system to realise I could fall in love so hard and so fast, and I was afraid of losing you. I haven't exactly been a recluse all my life, Julia, but I never knew I could love anyone the way I love you. . . ."

He bent and kissed her, that slow sensual kiss that sent her toes curling and her senses reeling, and the tingling flame of an answering desire running through her. He loved her . . . he loved her. . . .

Somewhere in the back of her mind something

struggled to be said, and she suddenly twisted her mouth away from him.

"What about Isla?" she gasped out. Before she lost every bit of control, she had to know the truth. There had to be no more secrets between them. "Fern told me . . ."

"You always keep on about Isla!" The swift impatience was back in his dark eyes again. "And Fern. Just what did Fern tell you, for heaven's sake?"

"That you were as good as engaged to Isla, for one thing," she stammered. "And she left me in no doubt that Rose would be very happy to have Isla for a daughter-in-law."

"And do you honestly think I'd let my family dictate to me about who I marry?" He was his old arrogant self again. She could have smiled, except that this was too serious a moment for smiling.

"Fern also said that you and Isla had spent a weekend together in the summer—"

"With about thirty other people!" Now he was really angry. "So that's it! I shall have words with that little madam and tell her a few of the facts of life. Unless you really prefer to believe her?"

His hands were running slowly up and down the curve of her spine. Through the thin, embroidered cheesecloth blouse she wore, she could feel the warmth of his fingers caressing her skin. She looked into his eyes, suddenly intense, and knew at once that he spoke the truth. It was Fern he was angry with now, not her.

None of it was true, then, and Isla was just another girl; even if she had once meant something to him, none of it really mattered anymore. As long as he was here now, with her . . . She shook her head slowly, and he kissed her again, more passionately this time.

She couldn't even feel resentment against Fern. She was only a child, for all her precociousness, and she'd seen Isla as someone very glamourous. All the same . . .

"But Fern's your sister," she mumbled. "And she's made it plain she doesn't like me. . . ."

"She'll change," he said positively. "Anyway, it's me you'll be marrying, not Fern. Won't you, Julia?"

She nodded wordlessly, the heady joy racing through her veins like quicksilver, everything in her world miraculously right.

"And just for the record," he murmured against her mouth, "I never was in love with Isla, nor she with me, I suspect. And once she finds I'm otherwise attached, she won't find it difficult to switch her devotion to somebody else. She's that kind of girl. Now let's forget about Isla, shall we?"

She leaned against him weakly, too emotional to speak.

"There's one more thing I want to know," Vince said slowly. "Do you love me? I want to hear you say it."

He caught his breath at the sudden blaze of adoration in her eyes. "I love you so much I can hardly think straight," Julia said unsteadily. "All I ever want is you, Vince, and how you never realised it, I'll never know—"

He was kissing her eyes and her soft tremulous lips. She felt his lips travel down to her neck and the hollow between her breasts where the soft flesh yielded gladly to his touch. The flames of desire ran through her in a sweet primitive longing. She felt her body arch toward him as if it had a will of its own as they sank down on the fireside rug as one person. Vince's fingers were pulling gently at the fastenings on her blouse. There was love in his eyes and an answering response in hers, and she let his hands and

185

his lips roam where they would, exalting in the fact that they belonged together at last.

"Just before I prove how much I love you, my darling, I want you to have this—" Vince said thickly. He had shrugged out of his jacket by then, and his hand reached into one of the pockets. He handed her something wrapped in tissue paper. Julia caught her breath as she opened it to see the silver brooch with its emerald blazing in the centre.

"The annular brooch—" she breathed, her eyes suddenly stinging. "Oh, Vince—"

"Don't you remember it's a betrothal brooch?" His voice was husky with emotion. "You and I will begin a new tradition, and a new Galbraith legend for our children. But right now we have more important things to think about, I think!"

"Oh, yes—" She let him take the brooch from her hand and put it safely on a small table. This wasn't the time for such things. . . .

The two of them were alone in Aunt Meg's cottage and she wouldn't be back for hours. They had all the time in the world for Vince to show her how much he loved her. She lay back in the cocoon of his arms on the soft fireside rug, feeling his seeking hands exploring her body and giving a small sigh of pure joy as she thrilled to the demands of his passion.

There was no more need for the resistance that had kept them apart for so long, Julia thought with a shudder of pure happiness. Her arms drew him hungrily toward her as her back arched to meet him. Their bodies fused together as if they were part of the same person, and for both of them the brooch was temporarily forgotten as passion took them to the heights.

Ancient legends had no place in their firelit heaven. The past was no more than a distant memory, and all that mattered to Julia was that she was warmed by the arms of the man she adored, and the fever of fulfilled desire claimed them both at last. It was the kissing time, Julia thought dizzily, as the rapturous moments touched them both with magic. The kissing time, and more . . . much more. . . .

IT'S YOUR OWN SPECIAL TIME

Contemporary romances for today's women.
Each month, six very special love stories will be yours
from SILHOUETTE. Look for them wherever books are sold
or order now from the coupon below.

$1.50 each

Hampson	□ 1 □ 4 □ 16 □ 27	Browning	□ 12 □ 38 □ 53 □ 73
	□ 28 □ 40 □ 52 □ 64 □ 94		□ 93
Stanford	□ 6 □ 25 □ 35 □ 46	Michaels	□ 15 □ 32 □ 61 □ 87
	□ 58 □ 88	John	□ 17 □ 34 □ 57 □ 85
Hastings	□ 13 □ 26 □ 44 □ 67	Beckman	□ 8 □ 37 □ 54 □ 72
Vitek	□ 33 □ 47 □ 66 □ 84		□ 96

$1.50 each

□ 5 Goforth	□ 29 Wildman	□ 56 Trent	□ 79 Halldorson
□ 7 Lewis	□ 30 Dixon	□ 59 Vernon	□ 80 Stephens
□ 9 Wilson	□ 31 Halldorson	□ 60 Hill	□ 81 Roberts
□ 10 Caine	□ 36 McKay	□ 62 Hallston	□ 82 Dailey
□ 11 Vernon	□ 39 Sinclair	□ 63 Brent	□ 83 Hallston
□ 14 Oliver	□ 41 Owen	□ 69 St. George	□ 86 Adams
□ 19 Thornton	□ 42 Powers	□ 70 Afton Bonds	□ 89 James
□ 20 Fulford	□ 43 Robb	□ 71 Ripy	□ 90 Major
□ 21 Richards	□ 45 Carroll	□ 74 Trent	□ 92 McKay
□ 22 Stephens	□ 48 Wildman	□ 75 Carroll	□ 95 Wisdom
□ 23 Edwards	□ 49 Wisdom	□ 76 Hardy	□ 97 Clay
□ 24 Healy	□ 50 Scott	□ 77 Cork	□ 98 St. George
	□ 55 Ladame	□ 78 Oliver	□ 99 Camp

$1.75 each

□ 100 Stanford	□ 105 Eden	□ 110 Trent	□ 115 John
□ 101 Hardy	□ 106 Dailey	□ 111 South	□ 116 Lindley
□ 102 Hastings	□ 107 Bright	□ 112 Stanford	□ 117 Scott
□ 103 Cork	□ 108 Hampson	□ 113 Browning	□ 118 Dailey
□ 104 Vitek	□ 109 Vernon	□ 114 Michaels	□ 119 Hampson